A single shot, Carter's last, sailed over Jessie's head, then all was quiet.

He'd be coming after her, no doubt about it. Her only chance was to put enough room between her and Carter so he thought she'd doubled back on the main trail. Unknotting the ropes around her wrist, Jessie began leading the horse down the Indian trail.

At dawn she came to the stream. Two miles down she saw him. The thick cords of muscle bunched and knotted at his back with every swing of his axe.

When she called out, he stopped swinging and turned.

"Help me," Jessie managed to say, not more than a raspy whisper.

Then she fell, exhausted. . . .

*　　*　　*

SPECIAL PREVIEW!

Turn to the back of this book for an exciting excerpt from the blazing new series . . .

Desperado

DON'T MISS THESE
ALL-ACTION WESTERN SERIES
FROM THE BERKLEY PUBLISHING GROUP

THE GUNSMITH by J. R. Roberts
Clint Adams was a legend among lawmen, outlaws, and ladies. They called him . . . the Gunsmith.

LONGARM by Tabor Evans
The popular long-running series about U.S. Deputy Marshal Long—his life, his loves, his fight for justice.

LONE STAR by Wesley Ellis
The blazing adventures of Jessica Starbuck and the martial arts master, Ki. Over eight million copies in print.

SLOCUM by Jake Logan
Today's longest-running action western. John Slocum rides a deadly trail of hot blood and cold steel.

→ WESLEY ELLIS ←

LONE STAR

AND THE
GOLD MINE

J

JOVE BOOKS, NEW YORK

LONE STAR AND THE GOLD MINE

A Jove Book / published by arrangement with
the author

PRINTING HISTORY
Jove edition / April 1993

ISBN: 0-515-11083-3

Jove Books are published by The Berkley Publishing Group,
200 Madison Avenue, New York, New York 10016.
The name "JOVE" and the "J" logo
are trademarks belonging to Jove Publications, Inc.

PRINTED IN THE UNITED STATES OF AMERICA

10 9 8 7 6 5 4 3 2 1

Dedicated to
Bill Harris

LONE STAR

AND THE GOLD MINE

★

Chapter 1

The train rocked and labored forward on the narrow-gauge rail. They were heading up into the mountains of pine. Jessie Starbuck leaned back in the thick plush of a chair and looked longingly out the window of the private railcar, thinking of Texas.

True, the Sierra mountains were spectacular, but she longed for the openness of the range. And then, too, the private railcar seemed far too opulent. Coupled near the end of the train, far from the engine with its soot and sparks, it was furnished like a hotel room on rails—all polished wood, brass, and gilt. And, as if that weren't enough, the sleeping quarters were done up in satin wallpaper. It was the kind of thing some Eastern banker would ride in between New York and Boston.

"I would truly like to know who would buy such a thing," Jessie said, lifting one long denim clad leg off a leather ottoman.

Ki, sitting at a burnished wood desk, folded a sheet of monogrammed writing paper into an intricate origami crane. "You did," he said.

1

Jessie rose from the chair, getting her balance on the undershot heels of her boots as the train entered a steep climb. She strode to the opposite end of the car and began studying the oil painting that hung there in an ornate gold frame. It was a reclining and voluptuous nude. She studied it with a critical eye as she pushed a length of her long blond hair behind an ear. "I just don't see why we had to ride in this . . . this . . ."

"Rolling whorehouse?" Ki asked.

"Exactly," Jessie agreed. "Do you know that President Hayes and General Sherman visited Yreka by stage? What's good enough for the President should be good enough for us."

"We're here because your mining agent rented this for you," Ki answered without looking up from his task. "It is not every day that the boss comes to town."

Well, that part was true enough. She had owned the Starbuck Mines for over two years, and this was the first visit she'd made to study the investment that bore her name. But Jessie could tell that Ki was growing irritable with the accommodations as well. His Japanese half, the part that always shone through serene, was starting to chafe under the unnecessary extravagance. And they had just left San Francisco two days before.

A tiny brass bell rang at the far end of the cabin, signaling luncheon.

Jessie winced at the sound. There was no telling what horrors the French chef would concoct. Yesterday, he presented a full helping of oysters, held on ice specifically for her. Later, when she peeked into the pantry, she saw enough supplies to feed a small town through a bad winter.

In the past she had dined at the finest tables in Europe, Chicago, and New York. And she would admit to enjoying the food. But here, the food never tasted as good. A thick steak, some vegetables, and fresh bread were what she craved. She had always held in contempt those ranchers and railroad men who squandered fortunes to bring Eastern big-city luxuries to the frontier. Their efforts seemed an affront to not only the people who struggled to settle the wilderness, as her own father had done, but common sense as well.

Now, thanks to her mining agent, Jonathan Ames, she had become a hostage to that same ill-spent opulence. She cast a long, suspicious look at Ki, who just shrugged and set the paper crane standing at the center of the desk. He looked like a man about to meet some unwelcomed fate. Above all, Ki hated French food.

Jessie hitched up her jeans over her slim hips, then arranged her gunbelt. The .38, mounted in the large frame with peachwood grips, had drawn stares in San Francisco. However, it was a comfort, as much for what she knew she could do with it as for the fact that it had been a present from her father.

The chef entered the room silently, wheeling in a tea wagon loaded with food concealed under silver. Jessie and Ki made their way to the front of the car and took seats at the small table.

The chef, well aware by now that he was wasting his artistry on the ungrateful, lifted the silver lids. For a brief instant, Jessie's heart leapt in her chest. There before her was a steak. Then she saw that covering most of the choice cut of meat was a yellow sauce that bore a striking resemblance to a particular brand of heel-fly ointment she'd tried on the stock a while back.

Across the table, Ki grunted and began scraping the sauce off the steak with a knife. Jessie followed

3

his example, remembering that the ointment hadn't worked worth a damn.

"You should talk to Mr. Ames," Ki said.

"Don't worry, Ki, I will," she replied, cutting into the meat.

They ate in silence, both lost in their thoughts. The chef returned then, carrying before him a heavy silver bucket, engraved with a hunting scene and trimmed with gold. Inside the bucket was a bottle. "Champagne," he said curtly, all pretense at hospitality having vanished miles behind on the narrow-gauge track.

Before Jessie could object, he set down two gold-trimmed, fluted glasses and proceeded to uncork the wine. After he filled both glasses nearly to the brim, he produced from his apron a sealed envelope and set it down so that it leaned against Jessie's glass.

She arched a suspicious eyebrow. The cook vanished back out into the tiny galley, dreams of returning to the San Francisco hotel he'd come from dancing in his head.

"Should I even open it?" Jessie asked, still not touching the envelope, which was the color of ivory and trimmed with gold. The handwriting on the outside was extravagant, all curls and loops.

"It is either his resignation or the bill," Ki answered, pushing away from the table without touching the wine.

Jessie took the envelope in her hand, turned it over to examine the blood-red seal on the back, and slid a long, slim finger under the back flap to open it.

"It's from our Mr. Ames," she said.

"I am not surprised," Ki answered, returning to his origami.

Jessie read the note to Ki. It was brief: "Miss Starbuck, My sincerest wishes that your journey has

4

been a pleasant one and your accommodations such that you have noticed no inconvenience."

From across the room, Ki grunted with disapproval.

"The wine you now enjoy has been selected with great care to mark your halfway point on the trip. Once again, I greatly regret that I could not accompany you personally, but Starbuck business has consumed my full attention at this point. I Remain, Your Devoted Employee . . ." It was signed with so much flourish and in script so large as to be almost unintelligible.

Ki grunted again, unmoved by the flowery language or the consideration of the wine.

"Very attentive, our Mr. Ames," Jessie said, tossing the note aside and taking a sip of the champagne. Against her better nature, she found it delicious. She took another sip. Before she realized it, the glass was empty. Then, what seemed like only moments later, she was upending the bottle, draining the last drop from it.

With the last of the wine gone, she began to soften toward Mr. Jonathan Ames. It was, after all, considerate of him to arrange her trip in such minute detail, even if she was paying for it. But then again, the new mining operation was paying off handsomely. In just a little over a year, it had more than paid for its initial investment.

Jessie rose from the table and made her way, somewhat unsteadily, to the velvet settee. The champagne and continual rocking of the train had made her sleepy. "I'm feeling just a little tired," she said, watching Ki with lazily slitted eyes.

A small gallery of paper animals now inhabited the writing desk—a small zoo grown out of Ki's boredom. "I'm not surprised," he answered without looking up, an uncharacteristic note of sarcasm in his voice.

5

Removing her gunbelt, Jessie dropped it softly to the floor and sat down, stretching out on the soft cushions. The last thought she had before dropping off to sleep was of Jonathan Ames.

Jonathan Ames had met her at the train in fine fashion. Tall and thin, with a head of thick black hair, he cut a dashing, if not outright dandyish, figure on the train platform. Two burly porters flanked him on either side, waiting to put strong backs to Jessie's luggage. And it seemed that they greeted the sight of her single calfskin bag with some disdain, even as Mr. Jonathan Ames took it as a sign of not altogether unpleasant eccentricity.

"Miss Starbuck," he greeted her, then bowed. "I've anxiously awaited our meeting."

Jessie mumbled a few words and relinquished her bag to one of the porters.

"And this must be your boy," he said motioning at Ki. The word "boy" hit her like a slap, though Ki kept all sign of offense concealed. It was not the first time that Ki, master of the Far Eastern fighting arts and her friend more than employee, had been mistaken for something less.

"His name is Ki," Jessie answered, bristling.

"Why, of course it is," Ames said, seeming not to notice Jessie's abrupt response. "Of course it is, fine name for a Chinaman-boy. Ki."

"I am not Chinese," Ki said with more politeness than was necessary. "I am half-Japanese and half-American."

"Of course you are, of course," Ames said, then turned his back on Ki.

Jessie turned, about to say something, but Ki's eyes told her not to bother herself. With any luck they would be rid of this fool soon enough.

6

But that was not the way it worked out. Each day a new gown appeared at Jessie's hotel room. And each night, Mr. Jonathan Ames had some extravagant entertainment planned. Waiters at the finest restaurants in town knew Mr. Ames by name. The newspaper carried small gossip items about him and Jessie, listing them as business partners. And the dining and drawing rooms of the best homes were thrown open to them for parties, where Jessie could listen to Ames along with the other men make their pompous proclamations over brandy and cigars, while she was tolerated as a novelty and not condemned to the outer rooms with the rest of the women.

All in all, Mr. Jonathan Ames seemed hell-bent on showing her a good time, no matter how much of her money he spent and whether she enjoyed it or not.

Jessie awoke at dusk from a sound sleep. Opening her eyes, it took a moment for her to realize what was wrong. The constant motion, the clatter of rails had ceased. The room was basked in a warm glow from the golden red of the sunset to the west and the yellow from the coach's lamps.

As she slid her legs off the edge of the cushions, her eyes sought out Ki in the shadows. Finally, she saw him, near the window at the front.

"Water stop?" she asked, mouth wooly from the champagne. Her head ached, too.

Ki turned from the window, craning his neck around. "I do not think so," he said. "We are not near town."

"Probably deadfall on the tracks," Jessie said, walking over to where he was.

Then the blast hit. The impact of it jarred the train back, sending Jessie stumbling a few steps to finally catch her balance on the edge of the desk. A moment

7

later the debris from the Wells Fargo bullion coach ahead began landing in splintered and charred sections outside the window.

"No, definitely not a water stop," Ki said.

Instinct brought Jessie's hand down, her palm slapping against a taut denim-covered thigh and not the peachwood grips of her revolver.

And then there were shots. First the load blast from the Wells Fargo 10-gauge, and then the return fire from smaller arms.

Ki moved slightly and a *shuriken* flashed in his right hand.

There were other sounds now, shouts and swearing. Two more shots rang out. Jessie ran for the gunbelt she had now spotted on the floor. She had just knelt toward it when another shot shattered the glass of the coach, the slug plowing into the nude in the gold frame.

Ki ran for the opposite end of the car and turned the lamp down as the front door burst open. Jessie rolled behind the desk as she drew her pistol out, her finger squeezing the trigger until she saw that the intruder was the portly chef, his face showing nothing but a bland display of profound disapproval.

"Get down, you damn fool!" Jessie yelled.

The chef did, falling forward face-first, a bullet in his back.

"Now, what we got here?" a voice at the door asked.

Jessie fired toward the etched-glass door, the bright tongue of flame from her pistol illuminating the car briefly. In the muzzle flash, she saw a fat, slovenly man, unshaven, gun drawn. Her bullet cleaved his head just below the brim of his tattered miner's hat. Chunks of hair, bone, and brain flew back in a fine spray of blood. The gunman crumpled to the floor, falling on top of the cook.

8

Pounding at the rear of the car drew Jessie's attention. Turning, she saw a man, rifle in hand, burst through the rear door. He was raising the rifle as one of Ki's *shurikens* sliced through his throat, releasing a thick stream of blood. The rifle clattered to the floor as both hands flew to his throat, hopelessly trying to stanch the flow. His face ashen in the dim light, he fell to the floor.

Up ahead there was more gunfire, and the train jerked forward. Ki ran for the door, his boots soundless as he went forward. "Wait," he whispered, then was gone.

The shadowy landscape beyond the windows was gaining speed. Jessie hunched down by the desk, pistol drawn. Then, above her head, she heard footsteps. Marking their progress, she aimed the .38 upward and fired. The footsteps ceased, but she heard no body fall.

Ki emerged from the private car into darkness. The next coupled car was the Wells Fargo. All that remained of it was ruins. Dynamite had blown the better part of its roof off. Two guards lay dead, a dozen or more bullet wounds in each and the one closest to the door missing an arm, blown off in the first blast. Their big-bore shotguns lay close by, unfired. The safe, its door blown off, tilted through the wreckage of flooring. Mail and paperwork littered the floor, blowing in drifts toward the back of the car.

Ki, *shuriken* in hand, moved past the dead men into the next car, a passenger coach. A half dozen bodies lay scattered about on the seats. The windows on one side were busted out from gunfire.

The next car was filled with smoke. The potbellied stove had tipped, scattering hot coals over the floor. Two-foot-high flames burned in the first two rows of seats. It would be useless to try to pass them to gain

9

the coal car. The train was gaining speed now, irresponsibly so. And Ki didn't have to see the engine to know that the engineer was dead or gone, the throttle tied back.

Ki turned to head back into the private car. But through the smoke, he saw the man, a tall, big-boned gunman with a Navy Colt in his hand.

"Now you just rest easy there, Chinaman," the man said.

Ki froze, seeing the big man raise the revolver.

"Hands up there, Chinaman," the man said, moving closer.

Ki raised his hands, keeping the throwing star well hidden.

"What you got there? Lawman's badge?" the man said, squinting into the smoke.

"Yes," Ki said, and flung the *shuriken*.

The star spun out gracefully from between his fingers and lodged in the man's left eye. The big man fired a shot, which splintered the wood between Ki's feet.

But Ki was already on him. Advancing quickly, he raised his right foot and spun. The heel smashed into the big man's face, sending cartilage and bone stabbing like a knife into the front of his brain.

Then the Navy Colt dropped from his hand as the big man fell to the floor in slobbering convulsions, a great geyser of blood gushing from his nose and mouth.

Ki ran past him, stooping to retrieve the *shuriken* from the shriveled eye as he passed.

It was then he felt it and knew that he'd been tricked. The train sped forward as someone unhooked the rear coupling. Racing through the passenger car and then the Fargo coach, he reached the rear door in time to see the private railcar slide back. They were on a grade, so the momentum carried the heavy car

10

forward, but still ten feet or more separated the car from the rest of the train.

From Ki's perch, he saw a half dozen men or more on the roof of Jessie's car. Then he saw a flash, as one of the men touched a match to a fuse. The gray stick of dynamite sailed past Ki's head and through the blown roof of the Fargo car.

As he jumped, he saw one of the sitting gunmen on the roof raise a rifle and shoot. A searing pain caught him in midair and scorched through his upper arm. Then he felt the hard ground rise to meet him. He had narrowly missed the hard iron of the rail, catching it only with his left leg as he rolled down the narrow gully. A second later, the Fargo car exploded in a rain of wood and steel.

Up ahead the train groaned and complained as the Fargo car jumped the rails, dragging the engine down into the gully with a horrible noise of groaning steel and splintering wood. When the boiler blew, it was with a hot rain of water, flaming coal, and steam.

Jessie heard the explosions, but dared not go to the window or door. When she once again heard the footsteps on the roof, she took her time, shooting up at the base of the brass lamp.

Above her someone cursed and fell, and a dark form dashed by the window at the center of the car.

Then there were the sounds of boots running and whispers.

"Better come on outta there, missy," a man's voice yelled.

She didn't answer.

When the windows at the front of the car shattered with gunfire, she emptied the Colt in that general direction, then hurriedly reloaded.

11

From outside someone let go with a shotgun, and more windows shattered.

When she saw a hand rise up by the window, a stick of dynamite at one end of it, with its fuse sizzling, she fired. The window shattered more, but the hand popped up and deposited the dynamite inside, the fuse casting an eerie glow over the car. Then another stick came through, from the opposite side.

In a flash, Jessie was running, heading for the back of the car. When she reached the door, she jumped, prepared to hit the ground with her feet moving. But strong hands caught her in midair and wrestled her to the ground, prying the Colt from her grasp.

There was more than one of them, but Jessie fought hard, kneeing one in the balls and raking her nails across the other's face.

They howled with the pain, and Jessie rolled away as the private coach vanished in a burst of deafening orange flame that had bloated it for the briefest instant, then sent most of the furnishings flaming out through the windows and roof. A moment later, she heard the remains of the coach roll and crash on its side.

Jessie was on her knees, making her way down the hill, when she felt a hand on her boot. Kicking back, she caught nothing but air. Someone grabbed at her again and she fell, rolling onto her back. When she came up, she was holding the little hideout that she kept concealed behind her belt buckle.

"Now ain't that just about the most ladylike gun I ever seen," a man's voice said.

Above the man she held in her derringer's sights, Jessie saw another one. Greasy blond hair hung down to the shoulders of his black frock coat, and he was smiling through a mouth of broken yellowed teeth.

12

The lever-action .30–.30 in his hands was the reason he was smiling.

"Now, you just blow ol' Walsh away or hand me the gun," he said. "One's the same as the other to me. 'Cause I won't have to dig either grave."

She tossed the gun toward him. He caught it neatly and deposited it in the pocket of the coat.

"Thank you, ma'am," he said with false courtesy. "And I'm sure ol' Lyle here thanks you."

"Carter! Carter!" a voice called from up on the hill.

"Down here!" the man with the gun called back, moving his head slightly over his shoulder.

Two more men appeared at the top of the slope. Jessie could see them clearly in the burning wreckage of the private car. They were young and dressed nearly identically, in baggy California pants and loose miner's jackets.

Then the other one, Walsh, began to move, warily backing off from Jessie and then rising to his feet. He was a big man, with a large belly that strained out from his soiled shirt. He'd gone some time without a shave, but now more than a dozen deep grooves lined his face where Jessie had scratched him.

"Damn, ain't she just a little hellcat?" the one called Carter said to the other with a crooked smile.

Walsh was already applying a filthy bandana to his bleeding face. "Damned she-bitch," he said.

"Carter, we got problems," one of the men coming down the hill said. "Carter, Lyle got hurt, bad."

Carter, keeping the gun on Jessie, turned slightly to meet the new arrival. "How bad he hurt?"

"Got shot in the foot real bad. He's hurting bad."

"What she take off him, toes?" Carter answered. "Man don't need but two, three toes."

The new arrivals were close now. Both were tall, rangy kids, not more than seventeen or eighteen. They

13

looked hungry, like starved wolves, and enough alike to be brothers, with black hair and pale white skin.

"Naw, it ain't like that," one of them said. "Went up through his heel. Got him good."

"Took his boot off, it was like pouring beer outta it," the other said. "That much blood. Messed up bad."

"Can he ride?" Carter asked.

"Don't know," one of them answered. "Maybe if we tied down on the saddle somehows."

"We gotta look at it," Carter answered. Then to Jessie, "Get up now. We'll see what you done."

They were halfway up the small slope when Carter bent to fetch a low-crowned hat he'd lost in coming down, then turned to the two black-haired boys. "You go out find that Chinaman. And don't feel no obligation to bring him back, hear? No obligation on my account."

They nodded and took off, running along the slope, through the brush.

At the top of the slope, on the other side of the tracks, a fat man lay wounded and rolling from side to side in pain.

"Walsh, you take this, keep it on her," Carter said, tossing the rifle to the other man.

Jessie watched as Carter knelt down beside the fat man. By the flame's light, she could see how she'd shot him. The .38 slug had gone up through his worn boot heel and through his foot to the ankle.

"What in hell you step on?" Carter said, smiling as he examined the wound. "You step on that lady's bullet?"

"Cart, it hurts, hurts bad," the fat man said. He was grabbing his leg just below the knee and rolling slightly from side to side, trying to stop the pain.

Carter rose slightly from examining the wound, still smiling. He turned his attention to the fat

14

man, addressing him directly.

"Lyle, listen to me," Carter said, his voice oddly gentle. "It ain't that bad. Won't even have to take it off."

"It's bad, Carter," the fat man moaned. "Gonna maybe slow us down some."

"Ain't gonna slow us down," Carter said, standing. "I got something for the pain in my bag. But I got something I need you to do. Tell me about that ol' gal in Candalaria again."

"Now?" the fat man managed through the pain.

"I do love that old story," Carter said, walking back a little. "Gotta talk up, though, so I can hear you."

The fat man's eyes were squeezed shut. "Well, she says to me five dollar and I says to her two," came the anguished words. " 'Cause I said I weren't gonna pay by the pound."

Jessie watched as Carter took three steps back to the trees, then turned. "You always were cheap," he said, then drew.

The gun was out of the holster so fast that Jessie thought her eyes were playing tricks. Then the hammer was back and he fired.

The shot smashed into the fat man's head just behind his ear, ripping off a large section of skull to his eye, then smashing into his collarbone and opening a nasty wound there. "Oh, Cart, don't . . . ," he said, hands coming up from his leg.

Carter fired again, and a bullet went neatly through the top of the fat man's balding head. He shook for a second, as if cold, then lay still. Jessie looked away.

Holstering the gun neatly, Carter said, "See that, ma'am? Man's gotta keep up his practice or he lets his friends down. Ain't that right?"

When Jessie didn't answer, Carter walked over to where the other gunmen held the rifle on her. "I said, 'Ain't that right?' "

Staring out at him with defiant eyes, she held his mad gaze in her own for as long as she could.

"Ain't that right, a man's gotta keep up his practice?" Carter insisted, now reaching out to grab Jessie's chin in his hand.

When she shook his hold off, it looked as if he were going to shoot her. She could see it in his eyes. But voices down the track drew his attention away.

The two boys were returning, running toward them. "Carter, couldn't find nothing," one of them yelled.

"Could be twenty Chinamen in there and wouldn't find 'em," the other added.

Carter turned toward their approach. "Probably dead. Leave 'im," he said.

When the boys were close enough to see the dead man, they came up short, their eyes wide as saucers.

"What happened to Lyle?" one of them asked.

Carter looked from them to the corpse and then back again. "Hunting accident," he said.

When the boys didn't respond, he turned to Jessie. "Ain't that right, ma'am?" he asked. "Hunting accident?"

Jessie didn't answer.

"Well, damn, I can see this is just gonna be a real pleasant ride," Carter said with no little disgust. Then, turning back to where the horses were tethered, he ordered, "Tie that bitch up and let's ride before every marshal from San Francisco to Gold Hill shows up."

★
Chapter 2

They rode through the night, the five of them, the horses picking their way gently through a narrow trail up into the hills. The leader, Carter, seemed to know where he was heading, though he didn't talk much after they began riding. Once every few miles, he would ease his mount back alongside Jessie's and check the ropes that held her hands to the saddle pommel. He did this without talking, without acknowledging her, as if he were inspecting a cinch on a fifty-pound bag of feed.

The two dark-haired boys rode behind, whispering to themselves hurriedly in low voices. Several times Carter raised his hand for them to stop, then sat motionless in the saddle, listening before spurring his horse on.

Jessie put their direction as northwest, but could not think of any town they might reach. They could be heading toward Gold Hill or Virginia City, but she doubted it. More likely was the prospect that they had a hidey-hole up in the hills. She still did not know why they had taken her. With their saddlebags filled with gold and government currency, they would have done better to divide the stolen bounty into shares and split up. Jessie knew she had outlived her usefulness to them. If a posse or law were on their trail, then perhaps they could have tried to use her in part of some bargain. But as far as she could see, they had gotten away clean with a small fortune.

Then, too, she wondered about Ki. The two young boys had not found a trace of him. But that didn't mean anything. She had seen the burning wreckage from the trail. He might have very well perished in the flames. Yet something told her that he was alive.

They made camp at dawn. A small clearing at the base of a rock ledge provided cover. A quarter mile down the hill a stream offered fresh water.

The four men dismounted, then ground-staked their horses, before turning their attention to her. And when they did, it was the big one, Walsh, who took it upon himself to help her down.

"You're a fine one, missy," he said, untying her hands. The thick furrows of ripped flesh where Jessie had scratched him had clotted over with dried blood. She knew they would leave nasty scars. "Kinda like a doll or something."

Jessie didn't answer, but when he reached up to help her down, his hands went straight for her breasts under the loose-fitting cotton of her shirt.

Jessie twisted away and lifted her still-bound hands up in front of her to block his reach.

"I ain't gonna hurt you," Walsh said, a thin line of clear drool forming at the side of his mouth. "Quit squirming like."

He brought his hands up under her tied hands and tried again for her breasts. Jessie moved quickly, bringing her left foot out of the stirrup and over the

18

pommel. When Walsh reached again, she kicked him in the chest, sending him to the ground.

She slid off the horse as the three others spun from where they were setting up camp.

"Even tied like a calf, she's too much for him," one of the boys said, laughing.

Jessie stood over Walsh, watching. He scrambled to his feet, breathing hard, and moved in on her.

Jessie brought her foot up and kicked him square in the balls with the toe of her boot.

The fat man groaned, doubled over, and sat down hard on the rocky ground.

Across the clearing, Carter and the two boys laughed.

"Little she-bitch," Walsh moaned and got somewhat unsteadily to his feet.

Jessie took a step back, wary of the anger that flashed in the fat man's eyes.

"Teach you to go kicking a man in his privates and all," he hissed.

He was moving in on her now, crouched low, his arms spread like a wrestler.

Jessie moved to the side, ready to kick out again.

From the other side of the clearing, the other three men were shouting encouragement to Walsh, taunting him. Jessie knew that they would probably not help their comrade.

The taunts were too much for the fat man. He jumped, arms spread out in front of him. Jessie did a quick side step, and the big man stumbled, sailing by her to hit his head on the fender of the saddle. He fell just under the horse, who did a skittish backward step away from him.

Grunting, Walsh rolled out and grabbed for Jessie's legs. She let go with another kick, catching him in the ribs and knocking a hard grunt from him.

19

"She's just kicking your ass, Walsh," one of the boys said.

"Let her try this, then," the fat man said, going for his gun.

But before he could clear leather, a shot rang out from the other end of the clearing. It plowed into the ground between Walsh's legs, just above the knee.

The fat man's hand dropped from the gun, his face frozen over in dull fear.

Jessie turned and saw Carter re-holster his pistol. "That's all of it," Carter said. "She kicked your ass. Kicked it fair."

"The hell it is!" Walsh complained. "The hell it is!"

"Don't make me shoot you in that fat gut of yours," Carter warned. "Nothing so pitiful as a gut-shot fat man."

Walsh rose to his feet again, mumbled something, and wandered off into the trees.

With a nod of his head, Carter ordered the two boys to bring Jessie to him. They obeyed like a set of matched hunting dogs, flanking her on either side and leading her across the clearing.

Carter gave her a good look up and down before speaking. "That's a damn sight better than I woulda thought," he said. "Now, I'm gonna make you a deal."

"I don't make deals with scum," Jessie said, meeting his steady gaze.

"You ain't heard it yet," Carter said, smiling. "Could be I'm gonna let you go, give you a fair share of the Fargo money and send your fine bottom back to San Francisco in a Paris, France, dress."

"I doubt it," Jessie answered.

"Then you would be right," Carter said. "But tell me how this fits you. You ride along for a day, maybe two, don't kill none of my men and I won't have to shoot you."

Jessie didn't answer.

"And I'll tell you this," Carter continued. "You move false again and I'll let ol' Walsh have you for a couple hours. He gets done with you, you'll want to be shot. Now, we got ourselves a deal?"

She nodded reluctantly.

"That's fine then," Carter said. "Now I'm gonna have the boys tie you to one of them trees so we can get some sleep."

Ki heard groaning, even after the fire died and the sun arrived with a gray dawn. He heard groaning and he thought, "I must help." Then he realized that it was his own groaning.

Ki opened his eyes slowly. From where he lay, partially buried under the rubble of the train, he could look up and see the shapely outline of a woman's breast. Then very slowly, he moved his good arm around and lifted the painting off his head. The heavy frame was made of plaster, so it was not easy to lift.

Now he could see the tops of trees and the gray sky. By moving his head slightly to the left and right, he could take in the train's smoking wreckage. If there were anyone else alive, it would be a miracle.

For a long time he lay still, then he tried to rise, but something was pinning him to the ground like a turtle flipped on its back. Looking down, past his chest, he saw that a section of timber, probably a support from one of the coaches, had him trapped, holding him solidly against the soft ground. Then, in the cool air, he felt wetness soaking through his left arm. When he tried to raise it, the pain shot through him like an arrow.

21

He lay still for a time, letting the pain subside, then moved his right hand down to his belt. Working his fingers deftly, he managed to pull the belt from the pant loops and bring it up. Holding it between his teeth and his good hand, he worked it around the injured arm and pulled it tight. The bleeding stopped almost immediately.

Then he waited, drifting in and out of consciousness. With each wakeful moment, he took quiet inventory of his injuries. Yes, he had been shot, as he remembered it with a rifle. But the bone in his arm did not feel as if it were broken. His legs, too, were crushed, but thanks to the soft earth, neither of them, it seemed, was broken. The worst was his head. It ached and throbbed painfully. Several times he reached around and felt tentatively for a wound, but could find none.

By noon, he awoke from a fitful sleep. Still dazed, he wished again for the painting of the nude woman to offer him some shelter from the sun.

When he heard the wagon, its heavy wheels crunching over the road, he began to shout. Then he heard voices; two men, maybe more.

They reached him after a long time. Opening his eyes, Ki saw two men, outfitted like miners, standing over him.

"Damn me, it's a dead Chinaman," the first said, scratching his beard.

"I am not dead," Ki said, groggily. "Help, please."

"What you think?" the other miner asked.

"If he's dead, he's the talkingest dead man I ever saw," came the answer.

A moment later, two sets of strong hands were pulling rubble from Ki's legs. When his legs were free, one of the miners asked, "Can you walk?"

"Think so," Ki answered, groggily.

Then they were helping him up, pulling him to his feet by the arms. Ki stood for a second, surveying the scene of horrible carnage, then fell.

When he awoke again, it was in the back of a large wagon. A Washoe wagon, he guessed, from one of the mining camps. The bed of the wagon was empty, and the miners had done the best they could to make Ki comfortable, using old sacks and a horse blanket. The wagon moved steadily over the rutted road, bouncing Ki a good deal. Ahead, on the seat, he heard the two men talking.

"Jessie, where is Jessie?" Ki asked, his voice dry in his throat. When he tried to lift himself on one arm, the pain in his head and the shifting wagon put him back down.

"Jessie on that train?" one of the men asked, turning in the seat.

"Yes, on that train," Ki managed. "I must find her."

"Only dead people on that train now," the other miner said. "Everyone was killed, except you."

Ki heard himself groan again, then passed into a tortured sleep. When he awoke again, the wagon was still moving. But he heard voices. People were shouting. And then they came to a sudden stop.

Several hands lifted Ki from the wagon's bed and carried him indoors. They set him down on a hard surface, and a thumb opened first one of his eyes, then the other. The withered face of an old man with spectacles and snowy-white muttonchops came into focus. Beyond the old man Ki saw a rough-hewn ceiling and a brass lamp with a green shade.

"How you feeling, boy?" the old man asked, his mouth tight with disapproval. "I marvel that you made it here alive, way them fellas bounced you over creation in that wagon. Imagine you hurt some."

23

"Hurt," Ki answered.

"Damn right you're hurt," the old man answered. Then he shouted back to someone, "Dorry, fetch me cold compresses. Much as you can carry. Cold as you can find."

"How bad?" Ki asked, groaning.

"Gonna stitch up that arm," the doctor said. "Gonna hurt bad, but it ain't nothing to worry 'bout. I were you, I would put my worry on that head. Might kill you. Abscess in your brain. Horrible way to die. Ain't pretty no matter how you look at it. Seen it plenty of times. Worst way to die, I'd say."

The compresses came then, and the doctor applied them to Ki's head. The chill water did nothing for the pounding.

"This ain't gonna feel good," the doctor said and poured a pitcher of cold water over Ki's arm to clean the wound. Soon, he was scrubbing it off with a rough cloth.

"Now, this is just gonna burn like hell," the doctor said as he poured a burning solution directly into the ripped flesh.

Ki gritted his teeth against the pain.

"And this ain't gonna feel any better," the doctor advised as he plunged a needle through a section of flesh and pulled the silk thread through.

Ki counted a half dozen sutures before the doctor bit the thread off between his large horselike teeth and bandaged the wound.

"I'm gonna tell you straight," the old man said. "You stay put in this room with the lights down. I'll be sending Dorry in to change the dressing and add water to the compresses."

"Have to find Jessie," Ki moaned.

The doctor ignored him, shutting his satchel with a click of brass. "Stay put and maybe that brain won't

24

swell up and kill you. Week, maybe two, and you'll live until somebody shoots you or you fall off another exploding train. Understand?"

"Jessie," Ki said, weakly, his head spinning.

But the doctor was already turning down the lamp and walking from the room.

★
Chapter 3

Jessie awoke at midday to the smell of coffee and frying meat, and to the thick length of halter rope that secured her wrists to a giant pine.

It was Walsh who was frying the meat over a small fire, turning it in a pool of fat with a stick. Jessie tested the rope that held her to the tree and found it secure. Some animal instinct registered in the fat man's brain, and he turned from his cooking.

"Look at you now, all awake and all," Walsh said. "Bet you ain't a used to sleeping like that."

Jessie didn't answer, but she stopped pulling at the ropes.

"Bet you more used to waking up in big beds," Walsh said. "Waking up in satin and silk and such." He placed the stick down alongside the small fire and lifted the pan with the frying meat from the flames.

"What you thinking 'bout now in that pretty head?" he asked, rising and walking across the clearing.

Jessie shot a look to the other side of the clearing, where Carter and the two young boys slept, heads resting on their saddlebags.

27

"You thinking about some hotel in San Francisco or Dallas?" Walsh said, standing over her. "Thinking about coffee in them little cups?"

"What do you want?" Jessie asked. "You'd be riding faster without me."

Walsh's wet smile faded, and he knelt down beside Jessie. "That ain't none of your affair. None at all."

Jessie felt the muscles in her legs tighten. If she could get him in front, then maybe she'd have a chance, kicking out. But Walsh was beside her, nuzzling her hair, sniffing at her.

"Smell nice," he said. "Like a ten-dollar whore at the beginning of the night."

Across the clearing, Carter stirred, his form shifting under the bedroll.

"What do you want?" Jessie repeated, speaking loudly enough to wake the others. But immediately Walsh brought his hand around, covering her mouth.

"Don't wake them up," he said, his lips right at her ear. "This here is our little party." Then he was fumbling with the buttons of her cotton shirt, working them with one hand.

Jessie waited, shifting her head slightly as the hand pressed harder across her mouth. He had three buttons undone, exposing the smooth slope of her breast. When she brought her head up slightly, she felt his little finger slide between her lips.

"You're a damn fine-looking woman," Walsh said, eyes fastened on the underthings beneath the shirt. "Damn fine."

Jessie opened her mouth as if to reply, then bit down hard. Her teeth latched onto his small finger just below the nail.

Walsh cursed, screaming as he jumped up. Jessie brought her teeth down harder, biting to the bone and then severing the finger. She spit the piece of finger

28

from her mouth as Walsh leapt to his feet, a trail of blood pumping from the foreshortened digit.

"Damn bitch whore!" he shouted, grabbing the injured hand with his good one as he danced in front of her.

When he positioned himself at knee distance, his attention drawn to the injured finger, Jessie kicked out and up, the toe of her boot catching him square between the legs.

The fat man let out a wheezing yell and crumpled downward, and before he hit the ground, Jessie kicked again, hitting him solidly in the left eye with her boot heel.

The three men across the clearing were awake at once. Carter already had his gun out and was aiming it toward Jessie. One of the dark-haired boys was shouting, "Lady's beating up on Walsh again! Lady's beating up on Walsh again!"

Carter let a slow smile pass over his face and holstered the gun before walking toward Jessie. He kept his hands raised in an attitude of mocking surrender, even as he stepped over the fat man who was rolling on the ground, one hand clutching his privates, the other, bloodied hand up to his ruined eye.

"Damn, but ain't you full of piss and vinegar," he said.

Jessie stared defiantly up at him, waiting to be shot.

But Carter didn't shoot her. Rather he bent down and picked up the severed fingertip. The nail at the end was filthy, dirt caked up under the nail halfway down. "Shame how some men don't care for grooming," he said.

"That pig attacked me," Jessie said.

Carter examined the fingernail closely and tossed it off into the brush. Then he pulled a small barlow knife from his pants pocket. "Myself, I do as my

29

mama always said, to keep clean," he said, opening the knife.

Even in the fading afternoon sun, Jessie could see that the knife gleamed, sharp enough to shave with.

Carter ran the blade under his left thumbnail, then examined what he scraped off before squatting down. "Good lord loves cleanliness," he said, then laid the knife blade flat along Jessie's cheek, right under her eye.

"Way I see it, we're all in his image," Carter said, turning the blade so that it rested on her cheek. "Man don't take care of his own personal grooming, doing the lord a disservice. Ain't that right?"

Across the clearing, the two boys stared, open-mouthed, their eyes bright with the expectation of blood.

Carter moved the blade slowly, from one side of Jessie's face to the other, passing it carefully under her eyes. "Now, I'm telling you this in fair warning," he said, leaning in close. "You try anything again. Beat up on ol' Walsh, anything. I'll cut you up so bad the good lord won't recognize your sorry ass. You understand that?"

Jessie nodded as best she could.

"That's good then," Carter said, then brought the knife away. A second later, he was reaching it back to cut the ropes that held Jessie's hands.

She brought her hands up in front of her, rubbing them at the wrists.

"Now, you fix yourself up," Carter said, closing the knife as he stood up. "We'll break camp in a little while."

As he walked away, he was about to step again over the moaning Walsh, when his boot came back suddenly and he kicked the fat man in the gut, eliciting a new series of moans. "You hear that, you lazy sack

30

of shit?" he said. "We're riding now. Get to your sorry feet."

"Cart, my eye," Walsh moaned. "I can't see nothing outta it."

Carter considered the man for a moment, then knelt back down. "Let me look at that eye," he said, yanking the fat man erect, then tearing the bloodied hand away from his eye.

The fat man's face was a mess, stained with blood from the severed finger and old blood from the scratches drying on it. He looked like the loser in some Gold Hill saloon brawl. But the eye was worse. No white shone in it anymore. It was now a blood-red orb, bloated so much it looked as if it were about to burst.

"Damn, she caught you a good lick," Carter said, then released the hand. "But what you worrying about? You got another one, don't you?"

Jessie came to her feet, buttoning her shirt. If she ran for it, they'd have her. She knew this crew wasn't above back-shooting.

"I'm gonna kill that she-bitch," Walsh groaned. "Lookit what she done to my hand." Then he exhibited the bloody digit, raggedly bit through, for Carter's inspection.

Carter, impatient with the whole affair, said, "Wrap it. We're riding now."

"We ain't eat yet," one of the boys complained.

"Eat while you ride," Carter said, then walked back to saddle his horse.

Ki awoke again in darkness. It was not the vague darkness of drawn curtains and extinguished lamps, but the full darkness of night. Then there were footsteps, which tensed his muscles. He could feel another person closer.

31

Shutting his eyes, Ki listened, hearing the sound of small breathing in the room. Almost like a small animal's breathing, fast and shallow.

"Who is there?" he asked, his voice calm and flat, but his body, battered as it was, ready to strike, to fight.

Ki heard a sharp intake of breath; then there was a slight shuffling. A foot lifted, then fell, then another. Whoever it was had taken a step back.

"Who, who is it?" Ki asked.

Another intake of breath, then, "It's me, me, Dorry, Mr. Chinaman."

It was the voice of a girl or a young woman. Ki relaxed. "Yes, what is it?"

She took a step closer, her feet moving cautiously. "Doc said to bring you towels," she said.

"Yes, then bring them," Ki answered.

"Need to light a lamp," the girl said. "I can't see nothing."

"Light it," Ki answered, then tried to roll over against the pain in his head, but couldn't.

A match flared against the floorboards, then rose, illuminating the hem of a faded calico dress, then shapely hips, and finally a face. She was young, maybe twenty-one, and beautiful. Her full, heart-shaped face was pale as pastry dough and smooth as carved ivory. It was framed by reddish brown hair. Ki watched as she puckered her mouth slightly in concentrating, trying to light the lamp on a small table. When she had gotten it lit, she trimmed the wick down carefully, so that it cast a lambent shadow on the wall and ceiling.

"Where am I?" Ki asked.

"Tanker," the girl answered.

Ki thought about it a second, couldn't think of it being on any map he'd seen. "Where's that?"

"Ain't a big town, like Minden," came the answer. "That's a couple miles north and east."

Now, that sounded familiar. "Near Carson City then?"

"Guess. Not near enough to suit me," came the answer.

Ki tried to pull his feet from the bed and find the floor with them, but the pain was too great. It felt as if his head would explode. With his first groan, the girl came running.

"Now, you just stay put," she ordered gently, easing him back down. "Doc said for you to rest," she said. "Said he didn't want no Chinaman dyin' in his town."

"I am not Chinese," Ki answered through the pain. "I am half-Japanese. The other half is white."

A moment later she was applying cool compresses to his head. "Whatever," she said. "You dying on him isn't gonna improve his mood none."

Ki lay back and felt her small, smooth hands apply the compresses. Soon he had drifted back to sleep.

★
Chapter 4

They rode into the night. Carter led the way, then
Jessie, then the two black-haired boys, and finally
Walsh. Carter, Jessie knew, might have been mad, but
he wasn't stupid. He rode slowly under the full moon,
letting the roan mare pick her way carefully over the
rocky trail.

Jessie knew now that it was not the bank notes and
gold stuffed in their saddlebags that they had been
after, but her. It had been her all along. That was why
they had not asked her name. And why they didn't kill
her as soon as they'd made their escape. Though she
did not know the reason she was still alive, or why
Carter had deemed her life more valuable than those
of his men.

"How long are we going to ride?" Jessie asked
finally.

"Till we get there," Carter answered without turning, his eyes steady on the trail ahead.

"Until we get where, exactly?" Jessie asked.

"Where we're going," came the answer.

Jessie could not see his face, but she was certain he
was smiling at this small morsel of wit.

At midnight or later, they turned down the narrow trail, their horses crashing hesitantly through the brush to a wide road.

"We'll ride this till dawn," Carter said. "There's another down the other side we can pick up."

Even by moonlight, Jessie could make out the deep ruts left by years of Washoe wagons. These were mining roads, the wider ones and the smaller. Carter knew the country, knew the mines. And they were, after all, not on the run.

They had gone two miles on the wide road when Walsh began moaning again. The moans came in long, agonized spasms.

"One of you ride back there, see what's wrong with him," Carter ordered.

Jessie watched over her shoulder as one of the boys reined up his horse and let it drift back to where Walsh was slumped in the saddle. A second later a match flared and the boy drew a sharp breath.

Then the match went out and the boy spurred his horse forward, passing Jessie and riding next to Carter. He spoke in a hushed, excited voice. "Carter, he's dyin'," the boy said. "Dyin' bad."

Carter, without pulling up on the reins, asked, "What's wrong with him?"

"Don't know," the boy answered. "Something busted in his head. That eye looks ready to pop out. Cheeks all swoll up red and purple blacklike. Can't talk no more."

"Thought he was quiet," Carter said. "Most quiet I ever heard him."

"He'll be a lot more quiet, we don't stop soon," the boy said. "He's dyin'."

"Go back, tell him we can stop soon enough," Carter answered. "Look at that eye again."

The boy slowed his horse by the side of the road

36

and waited until the fat man was beside him. Then he relayed Carter's message. A moan was Walsh's only answer.

"See what you did?" Carter said to Jessie. "You are just bound and determined to ruin my plans, aren't you?"

"Maybe if you told me what your plans are," Jessie answered.

"Miss Starbuck, I do believe you will find out in good time," Carter answered, using her name for the first time. "I do believe you will find out in good time."

They rode for another few hours, until the moon had set, then Carter pulled them off the trail at a bend. The horses were complaining now, tiring under the ride. But a half mile up the slope they came on a grassy clearing, surrounded by small pines, with a spring at one end.

It took both boys to pull Walsh from the saddle while Carter helped Jessie down. Her hands tied in front of her, he placed her against a tree with a canteen of tepid water, then saw to Walsh.

A few minutes later, he came striding back, grim-faced. "You just about killed that ol' boy," he said to Jessie.

Jessie didn't answer; there was nothing to say. She'd come across men like Carter before. There was no telling what would set them off.

The two boys were building a fire, talking between themselves.

"You boys, you keep an eye on her," Carter called to the pair. Then he walked off into the trees to relieve himself.

A light breeze was blowing, and the boys were having some difficulty with the fire. They didn't notice as Walsh rose uneasily to his feet. By the time they saw him actually walking, in a stooped and painful stagger, it was too late. He was nearly on Jessie.

When he was five or six feet away, the fat man drew his gun, holding it out in front of him in a shaking hand. Jessie worked her way up to her feet as the boys watched, mouths agape.

The first shot went wild, off into the trees. Jessie dodged left and felt the second shot slice the air near her left arm.

"Gonna kill you, she-bitch," the fat man mumbled.

His face was a horror, black and blue, the bad eye swollen blood-red and protruding, the good eye glowering at her as he tried to aim. Around his injured hand was a filthy bandana soaked and crusted with dried blood from the severed finger.

"Gonna kill you," Walsh mumbled again.

When he was close enough, Jessie half turned and let out with a Bushido kick. Her boot caught him dead in the mouth, ripping and uprooting a row of yellowed teeth, then spinning him around.

Jessie could hear Carter then, crashing through the underbrush. The sound seemed to bring the boys to life. One of them jumped Walsh, grabbing him from the front. The fat man fired again, and the boy fell back, gut-shot.

When Walsh turned back to Jessie, he was choking and coughing. Then he spit out a tooth, and the bloody gaping hole of his mouth formed into something like a smile.

Jessie moved into a kicking position as the wounded man brought the gun up again. Then there were shots. A half dozen rounds ripped into Walsh from in front and behind, sending him spinning and falling to the ground.

Carter stepped from the woods, gun still drawn. On

38

the other side was the remaining boy, holding a Peace-maker with two hands.

"What in hell happened here?" Carter demanded.

"Lady started beating up on Walsh again," the boy answered.

"And what about him?" Carter asked, motioning to the groaning lad on the ground.

"Walsh shot him," the boy said.

"You tend to her," Carter ordered. "Put her back in the saddle. We're riding."

"What about him?" the boy asked. "He's blood to me."

"Well, he ain't shit to me," Carter said. "I'll tend to him."

"Cart, don't shoot me, please," the groaning boy begged. "I just got to get to a town. Find a doctor is all. Just put me on a horse, let me go my way."

"Get her in the damn saddle!" Carter ordered the boy still standing. The boy didn't move until Carter reached for his gun.

Jessie was in the saddle, the boy handing her the reins, when they heard the shot. Turning, they both saw that Carter had shot him in the head. A neat hole between the eyes was leaking blood.

"Cart, damn it, he was kin to me!" the boy cried, then went for his gun.

Carter drew the gun on him, but Jessie didn't see where the bullet struck. She was already spurring her horse forward, through the trees, the branches lashing back as she raked the animal's haunches with her boot heels.

A single shot, Carter's last, sailed over her head; then all was quiet. She rode hard until she made the wide trail and crossed it. She continued fast for another quarter mile, then slowed to a steady walk down a slope.

He'd be coming after her, no doubt about it. Her only chance was if she'd put enough room between her and Carter or if he thought she'd doubled back on the main trail.

A mile downhill she came on another trail, overgrown and rocky. Twice in an hour she thought she heard a horse in the distance and picked up her pace to a trot. The third time, the horse stumbled on deadfall and turned up lame.

Jessie eased down from the saddle, listening, then unknotted the ropes around her wrist and began leading the horse down the Indian trail.

It wasn't until dawn that she came to the stream. There she knelt, drinking, and let the horse drink almost to its fill before moving on, following the water's downward flow.

When dawn came, she found the first signs of the sluices. They were small, crude things, and she led the horse around, continued on. Two miles downstream she saw him. Not even fully light, and he was working with his shirt off, his long brown hair falling just to his back. The thick cords of muscle bunched and knotted at his back with every swing of the axe.

When she called out, he stopped swinging and turned. His young, bearded face greeted her with wide eyes, and then a furrowed brow.

"Help me," Jessie managed to say, not more than a raspy whisper. Then she fell, exhausted.

Ki heard the footsteps again and ventured to open one eye. The girl, Dorry, was coming to him with a tin bowl. "Doc says you might take some soup, if you feel up to it," she said.

Rolling toward her, he saw that the thick covering of the window let an outline of light into the room. Midday, he supposed. His head no longer hurt quite as bad. The pain in his arm had diminished to a steady throb.

She sat down on the edge of the bed and brought a spoon from a pocket in her dress. "Beef soup," she said, bringing a clear portion out for him.

Ki opened his mouth, and she ladled the hot soup in. "What is this place?" he asked, now observing the narrow room for the first time.

"Out back of Mrs. Baker's," the girl said.

Ki studied the room more closely as he took the second spoonful. There wasn't much to it. A four-by-ten cubicle of rough wood. The roof slanted downward, toward the bed. A single door, crooked in its frame, hung on leather hinges in the opposite wall. There was a low table and a single lamp with a cracked chimney. "I'm in a whorehouse?" he asked incredulously.

The girl made a sour face and brought another spoon to his mouth. "Most people around here just call it Mrs. Baker's," she answered somewhat snootily. "Or sometimes Mrs. Baker's place. It don't make no difference, except maybe you should show some respect. Don't they show respect where you come from?"

"Yes," Ki answered. "They show respect."

"Where you from, anyway?"

"Texas," Ki said.

"Well, that would figure," the girl said, as if she had known all along. "That would just figure."

Ki took two more spoonfuls before speaking again. He bit into a chunk of fatty meat and chewed it slowly. "What is Mrs. Baker charging me?" he asked. It was supposed to be a joke.

"Don't know," the girl said, spooning the last of the soup and the final, second chunk of meat into his mouth. "Between you and her. Tell you, though, none of the girls would set foot in here, except to watch you sleep. On account of what happened in here."

41

"What happened?" Ki asked, sitting up slowly, propping his head and back against the wall. "I mean other than what you might expect."

"I know what you meant. But a girl got killed in here," Dorry said. "Shot by a gambling man she was supposed to run off to Virginia City with. Been haunted since."

"Haunted by a whore?" Ki asked, smiling.

The girl stood up from the bed, pouting. "I reckon they can haunt just as good as regular folks." Then she stamped out of the room.

Chapter 5

"Now you just rest easy there, lady," the man said, gently lowering Jessie to the bed.

But Jessie was not about to rest easy. They were coming for her. Carter and the one remaining dark-haired boy. "Look, we have to be ready," she said, struggling from his grasp and regaining her feet. "He may be coming."

"Just who may be coming?" the man asked, a hint of only the smallest concern showing in his voice. For all he knew, this crazy woman had wandered in out of the tree line.

"That son of a bitch who robbed the train and kidnaped me," Jessie answered, then crossed the room to peek out the shuttered window.

Nothing stirred outside. It was midday and the sun was shining. The only sound was the trickling runoff from the sluice.

"Look, lady, we're about a half milc from nowhere," the man said. "You're the first person I've seen in three months."

Jessie turned toward him, facing him in the gloom of the shack. It was a bachelor's quarters all right.

She could tell from the scatter of clothing, the crude furniture, and the stretched skins that hung on the walls. He was still stripped to the waist, his pants worn through to a shine. A wide belt of black leather was slung around his waist, and from the belt hung a large Arkansas toothpick in a beaver sheath.

Jessie watched as he turned his back and lit the lamp, then turned the wick upward to send a warm yellow glow over the room. The muscles of his broad back rippled, and his arms, still taut from work, shone hard and tan in the light.

"Now, lady, I don't know what your problem is. I'll help you any way I can," he said, then turned. And when he turned, she saw his front, the hard washboard stomach and the thick tuft of hair that spread across his chest.

Jessie stared for a long time, taken aback by the sight. "Do you have any weapons?" she asked finally. "Shotgun, rifle, pistols?"

He cocked his head to one side and pointed to the crudely hewn wood mantel above the stone fireplace. A .44-caliber Henry Repeating Rifle, a 10-gauge double-barreled breechloader, hung neatly on iron rail spikes against the stone chimney. On the mantel itself a gunbelt of black leather curled, displaying a fancy revolver with bone grips inlaid in silver. Jessie moved across the room and grabbed the belt down. She saw that the revolver was a Roger's and Spencer .44.

"You know how to use this?" she asked. "Or is it just for show?"

He crossed the room in three steps and grabbed the gunbelt out of her hand. "I don't know where you come from, lady," he said. "But didn't anybody ever tell you not to touch what ain't yours?" He put the belt back on the shelf, laying it gently across the wood. "Seeing as we haven't been properly introduced," he said, "name's Slyke. Brandon Q. Slyke."

Jessie studied him for a moment, then said, "Jessie Starbuck." She waited to see his face, how he reacted to the Starbuck name, but he'd turned.

"Well, Jessie Starbuck, when's the last time you ate?" he asked.

"Yesterday," she answered, feeling her stomach empty all at once.

"Then I suppose you need a meal," he said, and began to rummage the shelves near the fireplace. "Can't offer you much hospitality, you coming in unexpected and all, but you'll eat as well as I can serve up."

A few minutes later he had stoked the coals in the fireplace to a good cooking fire and was throwing pieces of salted venison, beans, scrawny carrots, and wild onions into a small pot with a few cups of water.

Jessie watched as he prepared the food, taking his time and working with an economy of movement. Every half minute or so, she returned to the shuttered windows and peeked out. Across the small clearing, past the five stumps piled together, and to the sluice and tree line, she saw nothing. By the time the food was prepared, she had relaxed enough to eat, her appetite back in full.

Holding the pot by its wire handle, Slyke lifted it off the fire and carried it to the crude table, where the lamp burned. There, he wiped off two tin plates with a square of flour-sack rag and set them down at opposite sides of the table.

Two homemade biscuits, from a tin that had once held sugar, completed the meal.

Jessie ate tentatively at first, sampling the food carefully. When she found it delicious, she dug in, devouring two helpings of the stew to Slyke's one. He smiled at her appetite, and she smiled back across the table, grateful for his kindness and admiring that he had not put a shirt on for supper. In some ways, she thought wryly, living alone in the wilderness could improve a man.

Carter followed her trail downhill for the better part of the day. It wasn't hard work. Someone on the run always left an easy trail. Easy to read as Bible verses. When he reached the edge of the clearing, he held his hand up for the dark-haired boy behind him to stop.

At the far end of the clearing stood a crude shack, white cooking smoke curling from its stone chimney. And there, hitched to a crude post next to a lean-to barn, was the horse.

The boy eased up behind Carter, reins in his hand. "There, there's the horse!" he whispered urgently.

Carter nodded, studying the sluice and the mining implements scattered about the clearing.

"We going in to get her?" the boy asked. "Drag her on outta there?"

"That's your plan, is it?" Carter asked, turning to the boy.

"That's it," came the answer. "Go in there, bring her out, and go where we got to get."

"Boy, don't ever let your mama worry about you hurting your head from over-thinking," Carter whispered.

"What is that mean?"

"Means as long as we know where she is, then we know where she ain't," Carter answered.

The boy looked at Carter, back to the miner's shack, and then back to Carter. "That don't sound like no plan," he said at last.

"It ain't supposed to be," Carter replied. "Now, I want you to do one thing and one thing only. Move on up the hill a bit. Find yourself a nice hidey-hole

46

and sit there and watch that house. Watch who comes and who goes. If she leaves, then you follow, but leave a trail I can find."

"Where you gonna be?"

"Gonna be sending a telegram," Carter said. "Be back in a day. Maybe two."

She came in carrying a small lamp in one hand and a chipped washbasin with purple flowers painted on its side in the other. Ki watched her move toward him, her face without expression.

"Doc said to wash you," Dorry said, setting the washbasin down on the table.

"I can wash myself," Ki answered, sitting up in bed.

"Can you change that dressing yourself, too?" she asked, pulling a new roll of bandages and a small blue jar of ointment from her dress pocket.

As answer, Ki offered her the arm, the cotton shirt-sleeve cut off just above the bandaged wound.

She ignored the arm and began to unfasten his shirtfront. When she had it all the way undone, she tilted him forward, pulling him gently toward her by the back of the neck. For a moment, he felt her breasts' firm swell beneath the washed-thin calico of her dress. "You ain't getting shy on me now, are you?" she asked.

"No," Ki answered as she slipped the shirt down over his shoulders.

She studied him with a critical eye for a long time—the lean, taut, and hairless torso that outlined every muscle. "Don't appear that you hurt nothing else," she said, folding the shirt and placing it at the foot of the bed. "Leastways, nothing I can see."

"No, just the arm," Ki said.

"Then let's look at that arm," she said and began unknotting the doctor's careful bandage.

47

The wound was a clean in-and-out shot between the elbow and shoulder. The doctor had done a good job of sewing it up. Dorry ripped a small section off the towel and dipped it in the warm, soapy water. She cleaned off the crusted blood, revealing the neat stitches. When the wound was completely clean, she applied a dab of ointment to both sides and re-bandaged the arm with fresh cloth.

"Thank you," Ki said, examining her handiwork.

"Thank me when we're done and finished," she answered, then dipped a larger section of cloth in the warm water. She began at his face, tracing its chiseled lines with an edge of the cloth around two fingers. Then she worked her way around to his ears, and finally down to his neck.

"Oh, you are a fine figure of a man," she said. "I'll give you that much. Maybe even more."

Ki raised a curious eyebrow and got a smile in return.

She began washing him harder now, rubbing the soapy water over Ki's chest and across his shoulders, feeling the hard muscles give under the scrubbing.

When she had cleaned his nipples for perhaps the third time, bringing them to erection, she leaned down and gave each one a soft, warm kiss. But when she brought her face up and Ki tried to kiss her mouth, she moved back with a giggle. "We ain't done cleaning you yet," she said.

She cleaned him right down to his belly, dipping the cloth in the warm water frequently, as she scrubbed away at his firm stomach. Several times her hands grazed across his pants front, as if by accident, pausing just long enough to feel his hardness growing. Then, the hand rested on his throbbing manhood as she began to unfasten his trousers. "We have to clean you

48

everywhere," she said, leaning in close as she opened his pants.

Again, Ki tried to kiss her, to reach out and touch her breasts, but she moved back. This time she rose from the bed.

"Lift up a notch," she said. Then leaning toward him once again, her erect nipples straining through the dress, she pulled the baggy trousers off him slowly.

His hard shaft sprung erect, and she let out a little gasp, but kept pulling at his pants. When she had them completely off, she stood at the edge of the bed, smiling hungrily at him as she folded the soft material.

Finally she retrieved the cloth once more. But she did not begin where she had left off. Kneeling at the foot of the bed, she began washing his feet, running the warm cloth up each arch and then down the sole. Slowly, she worked her way upward, her hands reveling in the feel of his hard, well-muscled body— from foot to ankle, to calves, to knees.

Ki lay back down, abandoning himself to the woman and her kneading touch. Opening his eyes to slits, he looked down as she worked her way up the inside of his left thigh, and he saw her face, even in the soft glow of the lantern, blazing with lust.

Finally, she reached his privates. The first touch of the warm cloth against his balls sent a thrill through him. And then it ended. Ki opened his eyes again and saw her dipping the rag back into the water. She worked the cloth slowly over his privates, her hand gentle and loving on the cloth. At times she bent so close, he could feel her warm breath, moist and panting across the tip of his shaft.

Then she was gone again. Ki, throbbing with desire, opened his eyes and saw her at the foot of the bed, standing outlined by the lamp. "You just got me all wet," she said, then held out a piece of dress that had been soaked in the washing. "All wet and in my good dress, too."

She was unbuttoning the front of the dress, chin down, working at the minute buttons with teasingly slow concentration. When she finally had them all unfastened, she brought the dress down over her smooth white shoulders, hesitated for a heartbeat, then shrugged it off.

The material whispered lightly to the floor, and she stepped out of it, naked as a jay.

Her breasts were bigger than he had supposed. They rode high and firm, with large, erect nipples. Her hips were slim and her legs long and shapely. Between her legs was a patch of midnight glistening with high-mountain stars of moisture.

"For all that, you're still not really clean," she whispered.

"No," Ki answered. "There is still a spot."

She crawled onto the foot of the bed, light as a cat. And, like a cat, just the tip of her tongue poked out between her full lips. She began just below his knees, licking him lightly, her tongue playing along his firm, hairless legs. He could feel her nipples, hot, graze along as she made her way upward.

Finally, he could feel her breath on him, and he let out a groan of pleasure.

"No, this ain't gonna hurt," she said, looking up with large eyes.

"No," Ki said. "I don't think it will."

"I promise," she whispered sincerely, then let her tongue poke out and tease the tip of his shaft across the underside. When she was finished at the very top, she worked her way down again, first with just a touch of the tip of her tongue, then laying it flat against the underside of his shaft.

When she tired of this, she brought her head up and giggled once more. Then, opening her mouth, she lowered her head slowly, taking his entire length into her mouth.

Ki let out a small groan, arching his hips up.

She stayed like that for a long time, his entire length buried in her warm mouth.

Ki reached down and found her nipples. Catching both between thumb and forefinger he brushed them lightly, stroking first with his smooth thumb across the very top and then working his way around.

She purred softly, deep in her throat, sending a vibration of pleasure through Ki's shaft. When she finally lifted her head, she did so slowly, moving her tongue back and forth as best she could.

"Oh, but I'm all wet, still," she murmured, straddling Ki as she held his shaft between her two soap-slicked hands.

He released his hold on her nipples and let his hand trace a smooth, teasing line down her belly with his fingertips, until he reached that patch of glistening darkness.

She moaned and rolled her hips as he toyed with the tangle of damp hair. Then, probing deeper, he fingered her moist loins. She quivered and rolled her hips onto his fingers.

If she had teased Ki before, now it was his turn. He moved his fingers away playfully, letting them skim the dark surface of the hair. Her hips rolled again, and she brought her entire body up, even as she held his shaft with both hands.

Ki let his hand slide back to her moist crevice and slowly worked the tip of one finger inside.

"Please, please, now," she moaned, quivering as he withdrew and then inserted his finger again. "Please . . ."

51

When she could take it no more, she rose high off the bed and with two hands guided him inside of her. When she sank back down, it was in a slow, single motion.

Ki brought both hands up to her breasts, cupping them, running the palms of his hands across the hardened nipples as she began to rise again . . . and then fall.

He could feel her tightening around him, feel her fingers digging into his thighs as she rose and fell with increasing speed. Each thrust fed the next and the next. He could feel the sweat cool on his chest, and see her glisten in the lamp's glow.

And Ki met each thrust, his shaft sinking deep into her. Her breasts rode in the same motion, keeping imperfect time as Ki cupped them in his hands. Finally she clenched around him and cried out. He followed a moment later, pouring up into her.

She held him inside for a long time. Then lowered her face to his. He kissed her mouth, feeling her breath coming in a half gasp. Then as he slipped out of her, she lay across him and he kissed her eyes, which tasted salty with sweat.

For a long time, she lay there curled up alongside him on the narrow bed, one leg over his. Her fingers traced intricate patterns along his face as he toyed gently with a sweat-gleaming nipple. Somewhere, far off, the whorehouse piano player ground out a lively tune and a woman laughed, deep and throaty with liquor.

"I guess you'll be riding soon," she said, eyes closed.

"I must find Jessie," Ki answered.

Then they both drifted off to sleep.

★

Chapter 6

Carter walked into the telegraph office and stepped up to the counter. He wasn't exactly nervous, not like some ten-dollar-a-month hand who didn't like the indoors, unless it's a bunkhouse. He was nervous because he didn't like places with names. Banks, stores, theaters, hotels, and such gave him a chill. The sole exception was saloons. He could stand saloons all right.

The way he figured it was once a man puts his name to something, then he was making the rules. And Carter was a man who didn't like to follow nobody's rules. Didn't matter if they were written down like in the Bible or sewn into a whorehouse sampler. They were inconvenient as hell. Always. Carter was the kind of man who liked making his own rules as he went along, and more often than not with his gun.

A young man in a green visor moved lively behind the counter.

"Wanna send a telegraph," Carter said. "Send it to Carson City, fastest way."

"It's all fast now, friend," the young man said with a smile as he pushed the yellow sheet of paper and a pencil across the counter.

Behind the young man, a telegraph key was clicking speedily and an older man, shirtsleeves rolled up with purple-black garters, was taking down the message in large print.

Carter stared at the paper and pencil, but made no move to pick either up. "Can't I just tell you like, what to send?"

A wider smile crossed the young man's face. He had seen this situation before. But no matter how often it passed his way, he enjoyed it. Maybe he enjoyed it more every time some uneducated, tinhorn tramp stepped up to the counter. There was an easy way and a hard way to handle it, depending on his mood. And today his mood was dark; the old man had been riding him hard. "No, sir, all got to be written down. Official-like."

Carter stared at the paper, the top printed with some words, then back up at the young man, who was openly smirking now. "You making fun of me?" Carter asked, cocking his head to one side.

"No, sir," the young man said with patently false sincerity. "Why would I make fun of you? How would I, sir, gentleman of your means an' all?"

Carter stared up at the ceiling, studying the brass lamp with its green shade, the same color as the clerk's visor. The clerk watched him, smirking. The clerk knew it was best when they said it. That's what he liked best, the way they admitted that they couldn't read or write. Not even their own names. Damn tinhorns should have paid attention in school. Sat up front. Listened to the teachers.

"I truly believe you're having a go at me," Carter said, lowering his gaze from the ceiling. "I believe that."

"No, sir, I wouldn't—" the clerk began. But before he

54

could finish, he was staring down the barrel of Carter's Colt.

"You calling me a liar?" Carter asked. "Calling me a liar to my face? Is that what you're doing?" Then he clicked the hammer back.

"No, sir," the clerk answered, all the life draining suddenly from his voice, as quickly as the color drained from his face.

"That's good then," Carter said, but didn't lower the gun. "Now you write what I say. Write it just as I say. Understand that?"

"Yes, sir," the clerk answered, taking the pencil and paper.

"That's fine then," Carter said. "This here is to Mr. Jonathan Ames. Carson City, Nevada. 'Mr. Ames. Stock penned and safe. Ain't missing but one mixed-breed head. The drive was harder than you said before. We gotta talk more money cash. Tell me what all to do. Carter.' You got all that, boy?"

"Mister, you're way over the words," the young man said, as he finished writing out the message in a hand so palsied with fear that the point of the pencil broke twice and the letters looked like chicken tracks. "It's gonna cost you extra. All them words."

"Read me back what I told you," Carter said. "Read it back just like I said it to you."

The young man did.

"Now, you send that out fastest way," Carter said, slapping a gold piece down on the polished counter. "Send that the fastest way, and when he sends back, you come to me directly."

"Yes, sir," the young man answered, still staring at the Army Colt pointed at his chest.

Carter, still staring the young clerk down, slid the Colt back into its holster, turned smoothly toward the door, and walked out.

Outside, it was growing dark. All those who had come to town for a day's shopping had long left. Down the street he heard the sound of a tinny piano and the laughter of men. It spilled from the saloon's doorway just as surely as the light inside spilled out through the batwing door.

Feeling the coins in his pocket, he strolled down the boards to the saloon, enjoying the sound his boot heels made on the planking. With any luck, he'd have an answer from Ames tomorrow or the next day. Then he'd be able to ride back to the miner's shack, take care of that idiot boy, and the Starbuck woman.

Slyke built the fire high in the hearth, throwing on thick lengths of sweet-smelling pine. The fire crackled and roared to a blaze, heating the small shack against the mild chill of the dusk air.

He was wearing a loose-fitting canvas shirt now, but even under the thick material, Jessie could make out the hard muscles that rippled with his labor.

When he had the fire to where he liked it, he nodded to Jessie and vanished out the door. Soon he returned with a redwood barrel, cut down below the second hoop. "This is all the convenience I can offer you," he said, apologetically, then vanished again out the door, this time carrying the cooking pot.

He returned, the pot cleaned and filled with fresh spring water. He set the pot on the fire and went out to fill the kettle. In minutes, he had every container in the shack filled with water and on the hearth. "Best I can do in the way of a bath," he said.

Jessie's heart leapt at the idea of washing in front of the stranger, though she could not puzzle out her own feelings, whether it was excitement or panic she felt.

When the water was heated, he carried it to the center of the room, where the barrel sat, using a cowhide

56

glove to keep from burning his hand.

The water just about filled the barrel halfway. "Myself, I usually wash in the stream," he said. "Expect that would be a little chill for you."

"I've done it enough times," she answered.

Slyke ignored her answer. He began digging in a chest near the bed. When he came up, he was holding a bar of purple soap wrapped in a piece of cheesecloth. "Fella came through 'bout six months ago," he said. "Traded me a box of notions, woman's notions, for a meal and a night under the roof. This is what's left."

Jessie took the soap with a slight smile. It smelled mightily of flowers.

"Then I'll be going," he said and crossed the room to fetch his shotgun. "Be back a little after full dark."

"You're leaving?" Jessie asked, more than a little disappointed as her emotions sorted themselves out quickly.

"Got some traps I got to check," he said. "Maybe find us some dinner."

And then he was gone, out through the door into the diminishing light.

The room was hot now, and Jessie could feel herself sweating through the cotton of her light shirt and under her jeans. She stripped down quickly, letting her clothes gather in a pile on the rough boards of the floor, then stepped into the tub.

The water was delightfully warm, though it barely reached her knees. Squatting low, she unwrapped the soap from the cheesecloth and dipped it into the water. Instantly, the room was filled with flowers. Splashing some of the water up on her, she felt her nipples harden in the air. Then they hardened more at the thought of Slyke.

She worked the wet material up her long legs, then over her smooth, white belly. Balancing on the edge of

the barrel, she ran the smooth oval of purple soap up
her thigh, lathering her firm muscles, then working
the lather in with the strip of cloth. When she reached
the patch of hair between her legs, she lathered that,
too, working in small circles as she thought once more
of Slyke.

Far in the distance, she heard the roar of a shotgun.
And then another, identical blast. The noise froze her
in place, but when no other shots followed, she con-
cluded that it was Slyke hunting.

Once again, she moved the soap in smooth circles
across her secret parts. A small shiver of pleasure ran
through her, and she closed her legs, clamping her
thighs tightly around her hand as the other hand came
up to toy with her left nipple, erect and tingling.

Then, reluctantly, she opened her legs, brought the
soap up, and worked it across her breasts and arms,
cleaning now as she continued to soap. When she was
nearly completely covered in lather, she stepped from
the barrel and knelt beside it. Her long, coppery blond
hair hung low over the water. Then she rose slightly
on her knees and dipped her head, submerging her
golden mane in the fragrant water.

She soaped her hair quickly and rinsed, before stepping back into the tub and rinsing the rest of her body
in the flowery bathwater.

When she was finished, she stood, shivering slightly
by the lowering fire and its red, pulsing coals. Looking
around the room, she spotted a coat of red-and-brown
fox skins. She pulled it from the peg on the wall and
wrapped it around her. The tanned inner skins
warmed her immediately.

When she turned from the wall, she stopped with a
start. There, standing in the doorway, two fat pheasants hanging limp in his hands, was Slyke.

"How long have you been watching?" she asked,

gathering the fox skins around her.

He stepped into the cabin, dropped the birds to the floor, and shut the door. "Just now," he said. "I didn't see anything, if that's what's bothering you."

"Are you lying to me, Mr. Slyke, to save my dignity?" she asked, stepping in front of the fire.

He shook his head slowly, maybe even a little sadly, then lowered the shotgun to the floor and propped it, butt down, against the wall. His eyes were fastened on her, held by the way her hair shimmered with the fire behind her and her eyes burned with the fire within her.

"Ah, but would you like to see more?" she asked, smiling now, her lips moist with expectation.

"Just what are you suggesting, Miss Starbuck?" he asked, a small, sly smile playing along his lips.

In answer, she slowly opened the coat, revealing her magnificent body. She held it open for a second, then dropped it to the ground. Behind her, she could feel the warmth of the fire, warming the backs of her legs and up her shoulders.

She could feel his eyes on her, feasting like a hungry man feasts at a table, groaning with unimagined delicacies. His eyes traveled every inch of her body, from her feet up her legs, pausing at the thatch of hair and then continuing up her smooth stomach and her large, high-riding breasts. She could feel his gaze as she would his touch, and it excited her.

He walked across the room to her, coming to her as a man in a daze. When he was close enough, he took her in his arms and held her. Their mouths came together in a long, hot kiss. He smelled of the sweat of hard work and the woods. Their tongues met and lashed, then they broke the kiss.

He held her tighter, nuzzling his head into her soft hair. She heard him draw in a deep breath and knew that he was smelling the flowery soap.

"How long has it been since you've had a woman?" she asked, her voice a breathy whisper in his ear.

"Six, maybe seven, months," he said, almost groaning.

For an answer she kissed his neck, rubbing her cheek against his beard, which was surprisingly soft. "Six or seven months," she repeated, then kissed his chest, which the open shirt revealed.

His hands went to her breasts, cupping them gently and raising them in his work-hardened palms. She felt his thumb rub lightly across her erect nipple, sending an electric thrill straight down to her loins.

Jessie kissed him again and lowered herself, her knees sinking into the soft pelt of the coat. She saw then, in the fire's warm glow, the bulge at the front of his pants. Opening her mouth, she took it between her teeth and bit lightly. His body tensed, knees bending slightly.

As she fumbled for the buttons on his trousers, he lowered his hands and ran his fingers through her hair. Then she had him free, his member popping erect from the opening.

"Six or seven months," she whispered, her mouth close to the swollen shaft.

"About that," he answered.

Jessie tilted her head back and took the shaft between her lips at the base. Gently nibbling, she worked her mouth upward along the underside, planting a dozen or more nibbling kisses across the throbbing member.

When she reached the top, she stuck out her tongue and circled the solid shaft. Then Jessie brought her head away and rose slightly, gently taking the shaft and placing it between her breasts. With both hands, she sandwiched the thick member between her soft

60

breasts, slowly massaging it, slowly and sensually.

Slyke groaned again.

Jessie lowered her head and took the head of the member in her mouth as she continued to massage it, letting her tongue run slowly around and around the top. Soon the entire shaft and the place between her breasts was slick. She released her breasts and took the entire length of his shaft into her mouth.

Slyke groaned, his knees buckling slightly toward her. Jessie reached up and held him in her mouth, her hands grasping the backs of his firm thighs, feeling the muscles beneath the smooth fabric.

When she let the shaft slide from her mouth, she brought her hands up, grabbing at his buttocks, fingers digging into the taut muscles. Then she planted one last kiss on the tip of his member and let it slip altogether from her mouth.

Turning on her knees, she bent down and presented herself to him. In a second, he was down on the soft fur behind her, inching up between her spread legs. Reaching behind with one hand, she guided him inside her wetness with a groan.

He filled her completely, staying utterly motionless for a long time before bringing his hips back and arching partway out.

Jessie moaned and wiggled herself back onto him.

He was leaning over her then. She could feel his hard stomach across her back, feel the strong arm encircling her waist to lightly fondle one breast.

Then, as if by some signal each had been waiting for, they began to move, she rocking backward and forward and he thrusting into her. They began slowly, but picked up speed with each thrust.

She felt his breath on her back, then her neck. Soon he was kissing her, gently biting her ear and neck as he plunged deeper and deeper into her. The spasms began far inside her. She could feel herself tightening around him, as if grasping to draw him yet farther inside.

And then she could hold off no more. She moaned, her arm collapsing under her, her breasts burying themselves in the soft fur of the coat, her cheek brushing the pelt as wave after wave of pleasure washed over her.

Soon he was moaning and filling her with warmth. For the briefest moment his fingers dug into the flesh of her hips as he spent the last of himself inside her.

And then he, too, collapsed. She rolled slowly over, keeping him inside her. His hand reached around once again to cup a breast warmed by the gentle glow of the fire. He kissed her shoulder, and she snuggled into him. With his free hand he pulled the edge of the coat up and covered them completely from the neck down.

As the fire crackled and sputtered, Jessie purred, like a contented cat, and fell into a deep sleep.

Jessie awoke at midnight to the smell of sizzling meat. Lazily opening her eyes, she watched him, naked, tending to the two pheasants over the fire. The birds had been cut into neat sections. He was cooking them in a large frying pan, mixed in with wild onions.

Jessie gathered the coat about her and sat up. He turned at her movement and smiled back at her.

Soon they were devouring the birds in front of a newly stoked fire. They ate with their hands, the grease dripping over their fingers and down to their wrists. When nothing but bones remained in the skillet, he took her hand in his and licked her fingers clean.

Jessie leaned in toward him, pulling the large fur tight around them. "I have to get to town," she said, staring sleepy-eyed into the fire.

"When?" he asked, pulling her tight, his hand toying at her hair down below, fingers working their way in between her smooth thighs.

"Tomorrow, dawn," she answered, opening her legs, letting his fingers inside her.

"Then we won't get much sleep," he said, feeling Jessie arch her back, pushing into his touch.

"Not if we're lucky," she answered languidly.

★

Chapter 7

Carter was blind drunk and broke. Emerging from the saloon, he staggered out onto the boards, collided with a hitching post, scared two drowsing horses, then fell into the street.

After much consideration, he decided that perhaps he was just two drinks past healthy, but a dollar short of buying enough sleep into next week. He would have had something left at least, if the hotel hadn't demanded pay in advance.

He rose, grinning stupidly, and turned to his right. Something hard hit his knees, and he fell, doubled over into the horses' trough, sending a slow splash of water out both sides.

Flaying his arms and spitting water, he finally managed to pull himself partway from the water. Then someone from the saloon called, "Where you swimmin' to?"

Carter looked up and saw the batwing doorway crowded with men, a few whores and serving gals edging between. All of them were smiling, their faces lit by the saloon light and the appreciation of another man's bad fortune. The fact a man tripped seemed damn fine sport to them.

"What you all looking at?" Carter yelled, and rolled from the trough, immediately muddying his clothes in the dirt.

"Some damn fool fell into the trough is all," someone called, and then they all laughed.

"Some damn fool likely to get shot," Carter called back and pulled his gun. Even drunk, the Colt came out with enough speed to frighten them back inside. "Maybe a bunch of damn fools get shot dead."

But the crowd had already gone, vanished into the light and music of the saloon before the fun turned bad. He was a mean type; everyone in the place knew it. They knew it by the way he'd called and cursed the bardog and cursed others' good luck at the faro table when he was losing.

Carter re-holstered the gun and rose slowly to his feet. He took a few tentative, staggering steps toward the bar, but the journey to teach those bastards a lesson seemed too far. Too far by at least eight or ten feet.

What he really needed was a drink. He needed a drink and his hat. Someone had stole his damn hat. Turning, he saw it floating in the trough. All ruined now, no use even fishing it out. It'd look like some sloppy miner hat by tomorrow.

Staggering down the street, leaning left, then right, he moved toward what he thought was the hotel. Carter had a plan. He was going back to that flea farm and get his two dollars. Then he was going back into that saloon and have himself another drink. Something to take the chill off. Something good, too. Make damn sure they poured from the right bottle. What he'd been ordering was Old London Dock Gin. But that wasn't what he'd been drinking. Whatever that old lying, stealing, cheating saloon was serving out of those fancy bottles with those fancy labels wasn't gin. More than likely it was Everclear grain spirits with something thrown into it for the taste.

He was halfway down the street before he found himself in near total darkness. Turning, arms out for balance, he looked back and saw the light from the saloon on the boards, and the hanging sign for what he knew was the hotel beyond that. Standing in the middle of the street, he saw ahead of him only the livery, its doors shut against the night.

Carter began walking, thinking that maybe now would be a good time to look after his horse. He moved steadily, concentrating hard on keeping a straight line. He was nearly to the door when he heard a voice behind him. "Where you heading, friend?"

"Gonna get some sleep," Carter answered, turning to see the vague visage of two men. Both were dressed nearly identically in shabby clothes and battered hats. Both were skinny, their eyes large in their heads, their unshaven cheeks sunken. They looked like they needed a meal and a shave. One was just a hair taller. The other was nervous and kept licking his lips.

"That there's the livery," one of the men, the taller one, said, easing up alongside Carter. "Man with fine boots like you got should be sleeping in a hotel."

"You trying to tell me where to sleep?" Carter said. "I ain't sleeping in the livery. Just got to see my horse. Her stomach's all knotted up. Gonna check her."

The second man came up along Carter's other side. "We didn't think no man like you would be sleeping in the livery like a hand. Not someone with a fine Colt outfit like you got strapped 'round his waist."

"Well, I wasn't gonna sleep in no—" Carter began to answer, and then stopped, falling forward.

"Easy there, friend," the taller man said, as they both caught him by the elbows.

"I got money coming," Carter said. "Lots of money."

"Don't say?" the shorter one said, as they both eased him forward toward the livery.

"Ever hear of Jonathan Ames?" Carter asked, turning from one to the other. They were supporting him by the elbows now, his feet lagging slightly behind.

"Can't say," the taller one answered.

"Big man, rich," Carter said. "Sent him a telegraph today. Personal and confidential business."

They were nearly to the side of the livery. Just ahead, beyond the alley between the livery and the assay office, lay an open field.

"What he do, this Mr. Ames?" the tall one asked.

Carter turned toward the man, nearly pulling himself free of the other's grasp. "Don't do nothing," Carter said. "Wears hundred-dollar suits an' silk shirts. Sits back and counts money."

"That ain't bad work," the tall one said.

"I'd take my share, if'n it was offered," the other one said. "Wouldn't have to ask twice."

They were right at the mouth of the alley now. Each of the skinny men swiveled his head up and down the deserted street.

"Where we going?" Carter asked, pulling suddenly free of their grip, then falling sideways as he gained the freedom. "Where we going?"

"We got a bottle back here," the tall one said.

"I don't drink no jake," Carter answered. "Been drinking jake all night. Don't need that."

"Not jake," the shorter one said. "Got a case of whiskey. Drove her in from San Francisco."

Carter stopped just inside the mouth of the alley. "Where would two like you get whiskey? A case of it."

68

"Drove her in from the warehouse in San Francisco," the tall one said. "Porter put one too many on the wagon. Been drinking it all the way up, ain't that right?"

"Honest truth there," the other answered. "Ain't got but maybe a dozen bottles left."

"Let's be at it then," Carter said enthusiastically, once again pulling himself from their grasp as he lurched forward.

They ran after him down the alley, catching up only when he stopped dead in his tracks, surrounded by dark.

They moved for him quick, the tall one pulling a piece of iron bar from his pocket. He had his arm raised high, intending to hit the drunk just behind the ear, when the man turned.

Carter took the blow square on the nose, the thick bar flattening it to his face and sending him to his knees as a fountain of blood flowed down his shirtfront. Liquor had numbed his senses. The pain was bad, but not as bad as it would have been sober. As he started to say something, the other man kicked him, the boot missing his stomach and landing square on his jaw, cracking it down the center of his chin like old wood.

Carter fell back, gagging on his own blood. Someone was pulling at his boots. When he went for his gun, another boot came down, smashing into his face and splaying the already busted jaw wide.

The world went white with pain as Carter let out a long moan that died in a gagging cough of blood. He felt for all the world as if he were drowning. Both his boots were off now, and someone was working at the buckle of his gunbelt. Another set of hands was searching his pockets. Someone cursed when no money was found.

Carter tried to roll over, pushing himself desperately with one hand. He moaned, and a thick pool of blood poured from his ruined mouth.

"He ain't got no money," one of them said. "None at all."

"Ain't there nothing in this world easy no more," the other man complained.

"This here is easy," his friend said, and pulled out a razor.

Carter tried to stir, seeing a glint of polished steel hovering in the darkness above him. A second later, he felt the razor cleave the flesh of his neck.

Then the steel appeared once more, and he felt it, brushing against his cheek as the tall one cleaned off the blood. It was getting awful cold, January high-country cold, awful fast.

"Well damn, you nearly took his head off," the other one said from a distance.

It was the last thing Carter heard.

Jonathan Ames leaned back in the leather chair in his office and read Carter's telegram once again.

The office wasn't much, not even for Carson City, just two rooms above an undertaker. But that's the way Ames liked it, very modest. Even the sign that hung outside the door—STARBUCK & AMES MINING—was the least expensive he could purchase. The less attention paid to the company, the better.

He read the telegram slowly, taking his time and thinking about every word. The way Carter had written it, well, it could mean a multitude of things, both good and bad. Obviously, the plan had not gone flawlessly. Just how bad it had gone, Ames was not sure.

He rolled the scrap of paper carefully and struck a match. When the paper was flaming in his hand, he rose slowly from his chair and crossed the room to

70

dispose of it in the small stove. By the time he shut the iron door to the stove, he had reached a decision. Carter and his band of thugs had failed. There was nothing to do but meet the incompetent and set things straight. If he had the girl, Jessica, that was at least something. But her servant, that Chinaman half-breed, could cause trouble.

Slipping into his coat, Ames exited his office and walked the narrow flight of stairs that ran along the side of the wood building. Two of the undertaker's sons were working in the shed out back, building coffins. The undertaker himself, a florid man with bright red hair, would be drunk and sleeping in one of the completed boxes nearby.

Stopping at the foot of the stairs, Ames eyed the two burly brothers with quiet contempt. They ran the business with a carefree attitude. Often they spent as long as two days building a casket, if the mood struck them. Cheaper materials, higher prices, and a little more enthusiasm for the work, that's what they needed.

One of the brothers ceased working and waved. Ames kept staring, then left for the stage office without answering. He would book his ticket immediately, then return to his quarters and pack. Obviously, there was no time to spare. That idiot Carter had probably ruined the entire thing.

★
Chapter 8

Stripped to the waist, hands out in front of him, Ki stood rigid in the early morning chill. His eyes stared straight ahead, in an attitude of perfect concentration. His mind was completely clear. A slight wind was blowing, flattening his baggy trousers to his legs. Though, even in the slight chill, he seemed not to notice.

Then, all at once he began moving, arms rising and lowering, feet kicking as he moved flawlessly through a martial arts form. The exercise took him from one end of the small yard to the other, then back again. The bandage on his arm did not slow his movements.

"Better come quick, Dorry," a woman's voice in the house yelled. "Your Chinaman's pitching some kinda awful fit in the yard. Scaring hell out of the chickens."

Dorry ran from the parlor room to the back window, where she peered wide-eyed out at Ki. "He ain't Chinese," she said at last. "He's Japanese. And only half-Japanese; other half is American."

"Well then, he's pitching a half-Japanese fit and still scaring the chickens and what all. What he doing anyways? It don't look normal. Not close to it."

"That ain't decent," another one of the women said. "Man running 'round without a shirt like that."

"Ain't nothing you haven't seen before," another one of the girls answered.

"Ain't the top half they usually take off," the girl replied curtly. "And anyway, it don't look decent."

"Looks decent enough to me," Dorry answered, admiring Ki's physique and graceful movements. He was moving from one end of the yard to the other, hands out in front of him, feet kicking.

The women watched him for a long time through the window. They watched him move through form after form, until a sheen of sweat coated his body and his muscles stood out hard and defined. Even when he seemed to be looking directly at them, he did not notice the faces pressed against the window, mouths slightly agape at the strange spectacle.

He paused after a time and picked up a broken broom handle. It made a poor substitute for the traditional *bo*, fighting staff. But it would have to do.

"What's he doing now?" one of the women asked Dorry, who had set herself up as a resident expert on the stranger's mysterious ways.

"It's too complicated," Dorry answered, transfixed.

Then Ki was moving again, swinging and thrusting the broken broom in front of him. It moved fast, blurring like windmill blades in a high wind.

"But it still ain't normal," came the reply. "That man do anything normal?"

"From my experience, he does most things better than normal," Dorry said curtly.

A few of the girls giggled, turning slightly to face Dorry for a moment before turning back to watching Ki.

When at last he finished, he strode over to the pump

and washed himself from a bucket. When he rose from his washing, he looked up, toward the house, and the faces vanished. The only indication at all that anyone had stood in the window was a slight movement of the curtain behind the pane of glass.

Ki was in his room, sitting on the edge of the bed, when Dorry came in. She was holding his shirt. It had been washed, ironed, and sewn, though a little blood still showed around where she had mended the sleeve.

"Here, I reckon you'll need this, if you're leaving," she said, handing him the shirt.

He took it, nodding at the tiny stitches in appreciation, both for her effort and the obvious skill it had taken to mend the shirt. "Thank you," he said, putting it on.

"I reckon you're leaving," she said.

"I must find Jessie."

"This Jessie, you in love with her?" Dorry asked, then dropped her eyes to the floor.

"Yes, but not as you think," Ki answered, rising from the bed.

"You could find work here," Dorry said.

Ki shook his head sadly.

"I paid the doctor," she said, brightly. "Worked an extra shift for the room, too."

"Thank you, but I cannot accept," Ki answered, then fished a small leather pouch from his pants and dug out a twenty-dollar piece from it.

"Ain't nothing to be ashamed of," Dorry said. "Lotta girls do it. Don't make you a fancy man or nothing. Winnie, a girl in there, she done it for a hand. It ain't nothing but a gift."

Ki thought on this for a moment. "Then, you will allow me to buy you a gift? A new dress."

Dorry blushed down to her ankles. "I reckon that

would be all right," she answered.

A short time later, they were in the general merchandise, Dorry standing behind Ki as the sales clerk brought down the best dresses from the topmost shelves. In the end, they bought two.

As they were leaving, Dorry holding the wrapped packages, Ki spotted a display of hoes. They were stuck blade-up in a barrel.

"These how much?" he asked the clerk.

"Them hoes, two dollars," the clerk said. "Solid ash handles. Sharpened steel blades. Can't wear 'em out."

Ki lifted one from the bunch, running his hands over the smooth wood. He was without weapons, except for his small *navaja* folding knife.

"I will purchase this," he said, once again taking out his money purse. "If you will be so kind as to remove the blade."

The dark-haired boy squatted in the bushes and watched, mouth agape. He was taking her near the sluice. She was naked as a jay and bent over the crude wooden gully. And the miner, with his pants dropped around his ankles, was behind her. Even from the bushes, a quarter mile or more away, he could hear the woman's moaning and see her large breasts swaying with each thrust of the miner.

The boy crept closer to get a better look. Eyes wide at the sight, he watched through the early morning light as the miner withdrew his member and she knelt before him and finished the job with her mouth. Oh, lordy, it was a sight.

Then they were both washing and laughing in the sluice's icy flow. Oh, she was some woman, the most beautiful he had ever seen. She was a far distance from those big-boned gals back home in Kansas. He looked closer and decided she was like a different creature when he thought of all those railhead and mining-camp whores he'd been with. Unwashed, with bad teeth and dirty fingernails—and damned if they ever moaned like that neither. More often than not, only time they smiled was when you rolled off. Rolled off or paid them.

It was a pity that Carter was going to kill her. It was like shooting the best-looking horse he'd ever seen. But Carter knew best. He was the sort that didn't make mistakes. The sort of fella you could learn from. Learn how to do things proper.

The boy watched as they finished their washing and got dressed again. Then they stood talking, the woman running her hand through the miner's beard. From his vantage point, the young boy could just about hear what they were saying.

"I have to find Ki," she said. "He may be hurt. And I have to get to the law."

"Nearest law, real law, is half a day's ride," he said. "After that, you got a two-day ride or better."

"When can we leave?" she said.

He scratched his beard then, thinking. "Now," he said finally. "We can leave now."

She kissed him on the mouth and they walked back into the shack together.

They left while it was still early morning, early enough for them to hear the birds singing their first frantic songs. The horse that Jessie had ridden in on had a split hoof, which half a day's ride wouldn't improve any. So they rode Slyke's buggy up the narrow path from the shack, onto the main trail.

The dark-haired boy, crouched in the bushes, watched them pass with hollow-eyed fascination. He knew where they were heading. No need to follow, like Carter had said. But Carter would be madder than a scolded cat if he didn't obey orders. So the boy watched them pass, then scampered back up the hill to where he had ground-staked his horse. And then, setting out at an even walk, he followed them from a safe distance.

★

Chapter 9

Jessie and Slyke arrived in town a little after noon. The town wasn't much; it was less than what Jessie expected. But at least it had a telegraph. Jessie climbed off the wagon in front of the telegraph office, noticing for the first time that Slyke had buckled on his bone-handled pistol. When he climbed down from the wagon, he paused, just briefly, to tie the gun down to his leg. He didn't make a show of it, not like some men, but tied the length of leather cord around his leg as naturally as some men button their shirts or pull their boots on.

Two men, loafing in front of the telegraph, watched with steady curiosity, then addressed Slyke with guarded greetings. In return, he offered only a nod before heading down the boards to the general merchandise.

Jessie paid for the message with gold that Slyke had offered her, drawing the nuggets from an old tobacco pouch. When she came back out on the boards, the men eyed her with the same caution that they had used with Slyke. She saw now that they were clerks, probably from the assay office or the Fargo station. They had that soft, untanned skin of men who worked indoors and who were not accustomed to messing their mail-order shirts or trousers.

"You Slyke's woman?" one of them finally asked, not able or willing to hold the question a moment longer.

The other stiffened, hissing under his breath, "Damn fool."

Jessie said, "Pardon me?"

"Ain't nothing, miss; you just go, make yourself at home," the hisser said eagerly.

"I was on that train that crashed," Jessie said. "Mr. Slyke was kind enough to offer a ride to town."

"Didn't hear nothing about no train," the first man said, pushing back on his thinning hair. "Nothing at all."

"Course we don't have no train, yet," the hisser said. "But you just make yourself at home."

Jessie smiled, sensing something wrong. The men were afraid. But not afraid enough to run. Something, some strange curiosity, held them in place, just as surely as if their laced boots were nailed to the boards. "I take it Mr. Slyke is a prominent citizen," she said.

The first man snorted. "I suppose if that's what they call it now," he said. "He wants to call himself prominent, then I ain't gonna argue with him."

Geniune fear flashed across the hisser's face. He flushed deep red, then whitened even more, the blood draining from his face like water through a sieve. "Miss, you just make yourself at home," he said at last. "You ride in with Slyke, ain't nothing nobody in this town won't do for you. That's a pure and genuine fact."

Jessie shrugged and turned, then began walking down the boards to the general merchandise. Inside, Slyke was looking over a collection of pick handles.

The clerk behind the counter was scraping and bowing like a waiter in a San Francisco hotel. Slyke, seemingly oblivious to the treatment, continued to weigh the benefits of a lighter handle against one with more arc to it.

Jessie watched as Slyke made his final decision. When he was ready to leave, the clerk summoned a young boy from the back room to put the supplies in Slyke's wagon.

"You thirsty?" Slyke asked as they were leaving the general merchandise. "Or hungry?"

Jessie paused in the sun, deciding finally that she was hungry. They hadn't eaten since leaving his camp that morning.

"Cafe across the street," Slyke said. "Guess my credit's good there for now."

They were walking across the street when Jessie spoke again. "You've got quite a reputation in this town, don't you?" she asked.

"People think what they want. People say what they want," Slyke answered dryly. "Not my place to stop them."

It was the way that he said it that told Jessie not to pursue the matter. Whatever this man had done in the past, she knew him as a kind, gentle man, and a good lover. She owed her life to him.

They sat on the bench seats in the small cafe, and it was the same story. The owner bowed and scraped and filled both of them with enough "sirs," "misters," and "ma'ams" to last a week. And that before they'd taken a bite of food.

When the food, two huge ham steaks, finally arrived, the owner hovered anxiously, wiping his hands nervously across the greasy front of his apron. Slyke seemed not to notice, offering only a small nod by way of recognizing the food or its quality.

81

• • • •

Jonathan Ames was about to enter the Concord coach when the telegram arrived. It was a piece of good luck, the way he saw it. So, Carter didn't have the situation under control after all. If the arrogant, illiterate dunce had done his job properly, then the Starbuck woman wouldn't be gallivanting all over creation sending telegraph messages. Rather, she'd be dead, and Carter would have those signed papers, selling off controlling interest in the mining operation to Ames. The ransom, which he'd always seen as a nothing more than a bonus he would pay himself, would come later.

Ames paused at the coach's step and thought. The driver's impatience or schedule meant nothing to him. Finally, and with great deliberation, he looked up and said, "Bring my bags down, immediately."

"You mean you ain't going?" the driver asked.

"How observant of you to reach that conclusion," Ames said and began walking away.

The driver cursed under his breath, tied the reins to the brake, and turned to untie Ames's bags from the roof where they were secured.

"Damn, that fella travels with more notions than a woman," the shotgun said.

"About as prissy as any woman I ever known, too," the driver said, pushing Ames's bags off the roof of the coach. The three bags had barely hit the street when he coaxed the horses to a fine trot with the end of his whip.

Ames headed back toward his office and then turned abruptly and headed for a certain saloon he knew of.

He found what he was looking for in the back of the saloon. The big man, Daniel Greely Quimby, was dealing cards to himself at a small table. He was a big man with a little man's name. Well over two hundred pounds, he wore a faded brocade vest and white shirt stretched tight over his stomach. With the outfit, he might have been mistaken for just another disreputable, overfed gambler, except when he turned his attention away from the cards and focused a pair of mean black eyes on you. After that, only a fool would mistake him for anything other than what he was, a man who had pursued violence as a profession for most of his life, beginning with soldering, then progressing through hired gun. Right at the moment, he happened to be working for Ames.

"Well, Mr. Ames, you decided you need somebody with a little experience for that job?" the big man said, dealing himself a blackjack.

Ames sat, letting his eyes rest on the cards and the big hands that gathered them back into the deck. "It would appear that Mr. Carter's services were less than adequate."

"Told you that from the go," Quimby answered dryly. "Didn't listen."

"That's entirely unrelated to our present situation," Ames said curtly.

Quimby shuffled the cards, bored. "It is, huh?"

"Precisely," Ames said, as if making a point.

"Unrelated," Quimby said, more to himself than Ames. "You sent that boy, Carter, out; he didn't do no job worth mentioning. Now you send me out, like you shoulda done before."

"Quimby, the facts of the matter are that I require your services. Immediately. I need you and four men to leave today."

"Four men," Quimby said, looking up toward Ames for the first time.

Quimby's deranged eyes sent a slight shudder through Ames. In truth, Ames was frightened of the man. There was something not quite right about him. He feared that not only was Quimby capable of savage

83

violence, but that he was a man who enjoyed it.

"Hundred dollars," Quimby said finally, still shuffling the cards. "Hundred now, hundred later."

"That's for you as well as the men, I presume," Ames said, already reaching into his pocket, which was heavy with coins.

"Both," Quimby answered.

Ames counted the money out on the table, but the big man made no move to pick it up.

"Well, there's your money. Take it," Ames said.

Quimby put the deck of cards down on the table, then slowly smoothed the edge with one large finger. "Put it in my hand, Mr. Ames," he said, holding out one hand.

"What?"

"In my hand, put that money in my hand," Quimby said. "I'm not some two-dollar whore."

Ames reached down, picked up the five twenty-dollar pieces, and placed them in Quimby's hand. The moment the weight of the coins touched the hand, it closed. The large fingers easily covered the last flash of gold.

"How does it feel, Mr. Ames, to kill a lady with money?"

"Just do your job then," Ames said, throwing the telegraph on the table. "I'll be along the day after tomorrow." Then he turned and walked away.

"And Carter?" Quimby called after him.

Ames halted, turned slowly. "He's no longer in my employ. Neither are his men."

Quimby turned back to his cards, lifting the top one from the deck. It was the queen of hearts.

★

Chapter 10

The telegraph clicked and clattered out the message in late afternoon. It read simply: "Jessica Starbuck killed in train robbery. Cease impersonation immediately. Starbuck & Ames Mining. J. Ames mgr."

"Bad news?" the clerk at the window asked with a small snicker.

"This is entirely absurd," Jessie said. "I shall see about this."

Slyke, who'd been standing behind her, asked, "Anything wrong?"

"Apparently, I've been killed," Jessie said, handing him the sheet of paper.

"Well, of course you're dead," the clerk said with a smug laugh. "Everybody knows that." Reaching down, he held up a copy of the recent Gold Hill paper. Her obituary was on the front page.

Jessie snatched the paper from the young man's hand. Apparently, news of her tragic demise had reached the paper just as they were going to press. Most of the story was devoted to what Mr. Jonathan Ames had to say about the incident. He went on at some length in relating his heartfelt sorrow at the unfortunate and untimely death of his respected business partner. Real tears were reported. Immediately following was an editorial lecturing and sermonizing on the deplorable moral condition and criminal elements of the territory, where Texas-rich women can't travel by private railcar in safety.

"Well, damn," Jessie said, reading the story anxiously.

"Tell me, Miss Starbuck," the clerk asked, as he accepted the paper back. "You always ride 'round in private railroad cars dressed like a man?"

Jessie was about to say something, but before she could, Slyke silenced the lad with a look.

Outside, Jessie said, "There's been some sort of awful mistake."

"Probably," Slyke answered, his voice hedging a bet of confidence against the growing certainty of doubt.

Jessie stopped in her tracks. "You don't think I'm crazy, do you?"

"That's kind of a difficult question," Slyke answered, pushing the wide brim of his brown slouch hat up with two fingers.

Jessie faced him head-on, her eyes searching his for an answer. "Here's an easy one then," she said. "Do you believe I'm Jessica Starbuck?"

"Same question," Slyke answered.

Jessie could feel the color rising in her cheeks. Suddenly, she was furious with Slyke for not believing her. "Well, I've got an answer for you, Mr. Slyke," she said, in a low hiss. "Just go to hell. Go to hell, directly!"

Bystanders were stopping now, staring. The entire small street seemed to have come to a standstill to watch the spectacle. It had been a long time, maybe forever, since anyone had talked to Slyke like that.

"I surely don't want to give these folks something to talk about," Slyke said, whispering as he reached for Jessie's arm, just above the elbow. "Come on now, we'll head back."

"Head back? You're joking!" she said, and slapped him hard across the face.

All around her, the onlookers let out a small gasp of surprise.

"I won't ask you twice," he said, anger in his voice.

"You'd be wasting your breath if you did," she answered and stormed off.

Slyke watched Jessie take her leave, striding down the boards. Then he turned and headed for his wagon. Someone began saying something to him in jest, but the sentence died as Slyke stopped to stare at the jasper.

Jessie was at the end of the boards, carried along by indignant rage, before she realized that she didn't have the faintest idea where she was heading. She stepped off the boards, a dozen pairs of eyes on her, then stopped. Thinking for a moment, she turned and headed back for the sheriff's office.

The sheriff watched Jessie's arrival, leaning against the doorjamb of his office. He was a tall man, but skinny as a post. His lean face held a pair of crafty lawman eyes. "Hell of a wallop you gave old Slyke there," he said in greeting. He was smiling.

"My name is Jessica Starbuck," Jessie said.

"So I've heard," he said, his smile growing wider.

"I'm not in any mood for any games," she added. "None at all."

He just continued to smile and grin at her. It was a look that she hadn't received in a long time. The kind of smile that men reserved for children, fools, and women.

"I'm telling you who I am, Sheriff," she said. "Are

you going to help me or not?"

"Ma'am, the good citizens of this town pay me twenty-two dollars and two bits a month to keep peace," the sheriff said. "Now, you want me to go into city money and send off a telegraph message to Jonathan Ames, up in Gold Hill, telling him that you're his dead business partner? A millionaire."

"That's right, Sheriff," Jessie said.

"After you just now got a telegraph message back telling you not to send no more telegraph messages?"

A small crowd was beginning to gather around them. Although they stayed at a cautious distance, they could hear every word.

"Sheriff, you usually conduct your business on the street?" Jessie asked.

"Either the street or the saloon," he answered easily. "If you ask me which I prefer, I might just tell you."

"Well, sir," Jessie said. "I conduct my business in private." And with that, Jessie walked passed the sheriff into the office.

The sheriff followed her inside with a shrug of his shoulders to the crowd.

Inside Jessie could see two men in the cell facing the door. They were dressed in nearly identical ragged clothes. A third sat slumped in a chair facing the flat-barred cell.

"Now, what is this business that's so damn important?" the sheriff asked, taking a seat behind a battered and empty desk.

"Sheriff, I am Jessica Starbuck," she said, approaching the desk. "I do not know how to make it any plainer to you."

"You got any papers on your person saying that's who you are?" the sheriff asked.

"I'm afraid not, Sheriff," she said. "The train robbers

took them. Whatever papers I had and my guns."

"You got anybody nearby I can send a man to see?" the sheriff asked. "Other than Mr. Ames?"

Jessie shook her head no.

The lawman was no longer smiling. His face looked weary, sad too. "Ma'am, you have to look at it from my direction," he said, avoiding her eyes. "You come in here telling me you're this rich lady, this Jessica Starbuck. No papers. No nothing. And with Mr. Jonathan Ames claiming that this Jessica Starbuck is dead in the papers. I just can't buy that. I can't buy that at no price."

The taller of the two men in the cell spoke up. "Maybe the lady wants to take it out in trade-like, Sheriff."

"Shut your damn mouth!" the sheriff yelled at the prisoner, his voice low and mean.

"Lock 'er in here. I do believe me she's the Queen'a England," the prisoner shouted back.

"Go ahead you, ragged ass son of a bitch," the sheriff called. "You'll hang soon enough."

Jessie watched the prisoner as he retreated slightly from the bars, but still smiled. The man in the chair made no move.

"Ma'am, you got any kin, anybody close by?" the sheriff asked.

Jessie shook her head no. And suddenly it dawned on her she didn't have any money either.

"Anybody you can stay with, other than Mr. Slyke?"

Again she shook her head.

The sheriff took off his high-crowned hat and ran all ten fingers through his thick head of curly hair. "Well, then, I s'pose we gotta figure something out for you. For tonight, anyways."

"Bring her in here with us, we'll figure something

out," one of the prisoners, the shorter one, yelled.

Something in the sheriff clicked and a brutal anger enveloped him. He launched from behind the desk and was across the room in two steps. Both prisoners retreated in fear. But as the sheriff approached the cell, his boot caught on the leg of the chair and the slouched man fell over, dead.

"Well goddamn," the sheriff said, the anger drained out of him, as he bent to pick up the corpse. "I'm awful sorry you had to see that."

Jessie just stared, amazed and repulsed as the sheriff wrestled the corpse back into the chair.

"Like to set up the victims, staring at them," the sheriff said. "Makes 'em think about what they done and all."

In reply, Jessie could only nod numbly.

"Only do it for a day or so," the sheriff said, groaning under the weight of the dead man. "After that, they get a bit gameylike."

As the sheriff lowered the dead man into the chair, the head flopped back, and for an instant Jessie was staring into the horribly savaged face of Carter. His slit throat seemed to grin at her like a second, toothless mouth.

"That's him! That's him, Sheriff!" she yelled.

The outburst startled the lawman, and he dropped the corpse to the floor. "That's who? Who?"

"That's the man that robbed the train!" Jessie said, pointing. "The leader."

"Who? These critters, they're too busy murdering," the sheriff answered, forgetting about Carter's body for a second.

"No, the dead man!" Jessie said. "He was the leader. Name's Carter."

One of the prisoners stepped up to the bars again. He was smiling. "Hear that, Sheriff? We killed ourselves a train robber! You got a pair of genuine heroes locked up, you bastard!"

The sheriff let out a sigh of exasperation and bent down to pick up the dead man again, this time accomplishing the task. "Listen, ma'am," he said, setting the hat on the corpse. "That man's name wasn't Carter. It was Brem. And he was a regulator from up north, not some train robber. Now, I'm gonna fix you up for the night, find you a meal, and a place to sleep. Tomorrow, that's gonna be your own affair. Understand?"

Jessie nodded slowly in reluctant agreement. All at once, she felt all of the fight going out of her.

Ki, riding a claybank gelding he'd purchased that afternoon, set out for the nearest town. His plan was simple. To ride to each town within a day of the wreck, searching for Jessie or the men who'd abducted her. They would need supplies or would fall prey to their own appetites for liquor or women.

It would be a day's ride to the first town. He did not like the idea of riding at night, but he had to find Jessie. And he had to find her quickly. The telegraph message he'd sent to Ames was more of a courtesy than a desire for help. He neither liked nor trusted Ames.

He made camp that night not far from the road, in a small clearing. He planned to start before dawn and arrive in town just after noon. With any luck at all, he would find someone who knew of Jessie's whereabouts.

Ki had just ground-staked the claybank and was preparing to start a small fire when he heard the slight rustling in the brush directly behind him. He continued slicing up a small stick with the *navaja*, ears listening intently. Then he heard it again.

Rising, he grabbed the ash staff and casually walked

straight ahead, as if he were going to relieve himself. His arm was healing nicely, but he was not certain he was ready yet for a fight.

He walked a dozen paces into the brush and then began to circle down the gentle slope toward the road, moving silently over deadfall and through bushes. When he had made nearly a complete circle, he saw the horse, a sorry-looking sorrel with a battered saddle. Someone had tied the rangy swayback to a small sapling. Ki passed the horse silently, extending a slow hand to pet it on the neck. The beast lifted its head wearily, looking at him with grim hope of better prospects. Then Ki was gone, and the animal lowered its head to the dried clump of grass.

Moving back up the hill toward the camp, Ki spotted the visitor crouching in the bushes. He was wearing baggy pants and a filthy wool jacket. His slouch hat was tilted far back on his head.

Ki crept up silently, staff out in front of him, ready to strike. When he was maybe four feet from the stranger, he said, "What do you want?"

The kneeling figure jumped suddenly up, then fell in a tangle of feet. A high squeal, like a broken axle on a wagon, pierced the night.

"Damn, Ki, what you doing sneaking up on folks?" came the familiar voice, as the figure rose.

"Dorry?" Ki asked. "Are you following me?"

"Well, I ain't out for no Sunday picnic," she said, removing the slouch hat and letting her hair fall free. "Figured you might need some help. So I took my savings, bought a horse and some gear, and came after. What you fixin' to cook there? And is there a lot of it?"

Ki lowered the staff slowly, letting his weight rest on it. "Yes, follow me back," he said at last, not sure what he would do now.

They went back down the small hill in silence, to fetch the girl's tethered horse. Then they returned to Ki's camp. On the way, Ki noticed that two large, battered suitcases, the kind you'd find in a city pawnshop, were fastened to the animal like oversize saddlebags.

Dorry followed Ki through the brush, talking the entire time. "I just knew I did the right thing, following you and all."

"And you know this, how?" Ki asked, taking up his position by the unlit fire.

"Well, appears you need some help, is all," Dorry said. "Could see that, even before you left. So, I just packed up and left."

"Tomorrow morning, you will pack up and return," Ki said, putting a match to the kindling.

"Return to where?" she asked. "It ain't like it was a hotel back there. Once you leave, you've left. For good."

A small wisp of white smoke appeared, and soon the fire was a small blaze. Ki fed it larger pieces of wood, building it into something to cook over.

"Here, let me do that," Dorry said. "You're doing it all wrong." Soon she was stacking on enough wood to cook a full-grown ox.

"You are making it too large," Ki advised. "Much too large for cooking."

"It won't be too large in an hour or so," she answered, then turned to Ki with a wicked smile.

Ki did not question what she had planned for the next hour. Her smile answered every question and made a few promises as well.

Ki reached out and placed his hand on her breast. Even through the rough material of the shirt she wore, he could feel its firmness fill his hand. The stout little nipple rose under his gentle manipulations.

Dorry moaned and lay down on her side, her face

93

lustful and expectant. "I just couldn't let you go," she whispered, her voice as soft as the crackling fire. "Just couldn't."

"We shall see," Ki answered, and began unbuttoning the shirt. Underneath she wore a light cotton shift. Even on her side, her breasts swelled under the material.

Dorry closed her eyes and parted her lips. Ki kissed her full, letting his tongue wander into her moist, hot mouth and toy with hers.

As they broke the kiss, Dorry opened her eyes just a bit. "That's something I never let them do," she sighed. "Never let a customer kiss me." Then she raised her hand and traced a gentle design across Ki's face, her fingertips tracing slowly, from lips to ear, then mouth.

Ki leaned over and kissed her again, gently rolling her onto her back. Soon he was working at the belt buckle of the baggy canvas pants, then at the buttons.

When he had the pants undone, he rose back up, crawling between her legs, and began kissing her. He started on her mouth, planting a teasing kiss on her lips, then moved down to her chin, and neck. When his lips came to the swell of her breasts under the shift, he kissed each soft slope.

Dorry purred like a cat and shrugged the shirt off her shoulders. Ki kissed her gently, running his lips from her neck, across her collarbone, then to her shoulders. When he reached the sloping white softness of her shoulder, he pulled down the narrow band of material that held the garment up, and kissed the spot where it had rested.

"Oh, Mr. Ki, please," she purred.

He moved to the other shoulder and repeated the process. Then he worked his way back across, to the hollow of her neck and down between her breasts.

She shrugged her arms from the shirt and shift, releasing her large breasts from their confinement. Ki bent between them, feeling their fullness against his cheeks. Then, rising just slightly, he turned his head and let his mouth wander across her left breast to the hardened nipple.

"Oh, Mr. Ki, I'm so glad I followed," she moaned.

Ki took the nipple gently between his lips and held it there for just a moment, before teasing it back and forth with his tongue. She moaned again and lifted herself off the ground to rub into his leg.

Releasing the wet nipple to the cool air, he took the other in his mouth, teasing it with his tongue and biting it gently.

She was squirming now, lifting her bottom off the ground in slow, sensual gyrations.

Almost reluctantly Ki released the breast from between his lips. Then he was kissing her lower, working his tongue between her breasts, and slowly downward.

As he moved down, his tongue teasing and stroking at her firm flesh, she reached out and ran her hands through his straight black hair, toying with it as she moaned at the pleasure he gave her.

When he reached her navel, she let out a small giggle and lifted her hips. Ki pulled down, grabbing her undergarments and pants with both hands. She wiggled slightly as the canvas material slid easily over her full hips to expose her smooth thighs and the dark patch between them.

Dorry toed off her boot and lifted one leg, bending it so the knee was almost to her chin. When she extended it out again, she had released her leg from the pants.

Ki flattened himself out on the ground as she spread her legs wide. Then, very carefully, he lowered himself to her thatch. He began very slowly, his lips teasing lightly across the tops of the sweet-scented hair. But soon he was taking small portions of it between his lips and pulling gently. He worked his way down and around.

"Oh, please, please, Mr. Ki," she moaned, lifting her thatch toward his face.

When Ki stuck just his tongue between the full, pouty lips, it was like a flame igniting. Her entire body stiffened and trembled under his touch. He worked his tongue slowly from the bottom to the top, poking and retreating. With each touch she moaned and lifted herself up to drive his tongue deeper into her.

"Now, please, I want you, now," she said with a voice of purest urgency. "I want you inside me now."

Ki rose from the enjoyable task and, kneeling between her legs, unfastened his pants. She helped him with anxious hands, reaching out to fumble at the buttons. When his member sprang free, she took it in her soft, opened palm and massaged him gently before guiding him into her wetness.

He rested inside of her for what seemed like a long time. When he moved, it was in one long outward stroke that brought all but the very tip of his member from within her moistness. Then, very slowly, he pushed forward again, feeling her envelop him.

In no time at all, he was stroking steadily, in and out of her, his swollen member slick and cool in the night air as it pulled from her dampness. She guided him surely, with just her fingertips on his hips.

Lowering himself on a downward stroke, he let his head rest between her breasts, then turned his head slightly and took one of the hardened nipples in his mouth.

Dropping one hand from his waist, she reached forward and caught his sac in the palm of her hand.

Then, very gently, she toyed with it, using just her fingertips.

Ki lifted his head from the glistening nipple and opened his eyes. She was biting down hard on her lower lip. Inside of her, Ki could feel her clenching and contracting.

"Yes, yes, yes," she moaned, bringing both hands up now to rake across Ki's back, urging him to thrust into her faster and faster.

Ki obliged, feeling her hands tighten across his muscles. And then he knew that he was close, too. She pulled him in with surprising strength and let out one final groan as he released inside of her.

When he was finished, he lay atop her for a long time, feeling himself shrink within her wetness. Finally he rolled off.

"Oh, Mr. Ki, you are the best," she said. "I mean that, and I speak from experience."

"Thank you," Ki answered, noting that Dorry had been correct. The fire now was just right for cooking.

★

Chapter 11

Slyke was halfway out of town when he decided to turn the wagon around. It was that woman who had him all confused, but what he did was tell himself that there was no use to a night ride on that road and he'd be better to start out at dawn. He told himself that as he pulled into the livery and paid for the night. He even told himself that as he walked back through the center of town, nodding and howdying to folks. And he was still telling himself that when he pushed through the doors of the saloon. It wasn't until the fourth or fifth drink that he decided to tell himself the truth, and by then, it didn't matter. (By the fourth or fifth drink he was already half-drunk and not much mattered.)

By the sixth drink, he was feeling pretty low. And the kid making a helluva racket down the bar didn't help matters any. The kid was spending money and bragging, but not doing enough of the first to make the second less annoying, even to the bartender.

"You all here are looking at a rich man," the kid shouted as he bought another round for the men at the bar.

"Ain't nothing in this town I can't buy," the kid

said. "Liquor or women, I want the best."

A couple of the men at the bar were half urging him on, fearful that the free drinking would stop if they didn't. But Slyke knew the kid would spend until he was broke, then wake up in the back room without enough money in his pockets for a shave or a two-bit breakfast. That's the way they were, most of these young ones that come down from the hills.

Slyke hunched over his drink at the end of the bar. If his ears had had hinges, he would have shut them against the kid's yammering. When the bartender wearily stepped down with a bottle and nodded that the kid was buying, Slyke shook his head no. Don't take a drink from someone you're not prepared to like, that was his feeling.

Suddenly the kid's yapping stopped and so did the laughter the free drinks at the other end of the bar had caused. "You, down there," the kid yelled at Slyke. "What's matter, I ain't good enough for you to drink with?"

When Slyke didn't reply, the kid broke free from a loose knot of bystanders and strode over. "You, I'm talking to you," the kid said.

"Easy, Mr. Slyke," the bardog whispered from the side of his mouth. "Just a kid."

Slyke rose slightly and turned to face the boy. When the kid saw that it was the miner who'd been with that Starbuck woman, he came up short, but then quickly recovered.

"What's wrong, you two-bit tin-panning son of a bitch, I ain't good enough to drink with?" the kid yelled. He'd expected laughter from his new friends at the other end of the bar, but instead, he heard only a low intake of collective breath. Someone retreated out the back door, letting it slam as he vanished into the alley.

100

"Son, why don't you just go back to the other end of the bar and finish drinking your money away?" Slyke said in a low, calm voice.

The kid would have done just that, too, except he remembered what Carter had told him once, about never backing down from a man who insults you. No matter how big.

"What you do with your money, hide it under a tree?" the kid asked, drunkenly. "Or maybe you just plant it outright, hoping it'll grow."

"Either way, no concern of yours," Slyke answered, then turned back to his drink.

The bardog and the rest of the saloon let out a sigh of relief. But the kid was too dumb or drunk or both to know when to quit it. He took Slyke's turning back toward the drink as a sign of cowardice. Smiling, he reached out and put a hand on Slyke's shoulder.

"I'm talking to you!" he slurred, trying to pull Slyke around.

Slyke dropped his shoulder and rolled it, so the kid lost his grip and staggered back. "You're drunk enough," Slyke said, still not turning away. "Best find some place to sleep it off."

The kid came to his feet unsteadily, a mean snarl spreading across his lips. "You think I'm trash, don't you, you bastard?" he growled.

"Son, I don't know you," Slyke answered.

"Leave off it, kid," someone down at the end of the bar shouted.

The kid moved toward Slyke again, trying to grab him with two hands and turn him. "Look at me when I'm talking," he demanded.

But Slyke moved faster. He turned quickly, fists up, and cut a good punch into the kid's gut, sending him staggering back.

The kid, gasping, regained his balance against a

101

table and pushed forward, coming back for more. Slyke snaked out a left and caught him on the chin, sending him back to the empty table, this time overturning it. "Now, you just leave off, kid," Slyke said.

"You tin-panning, gravel-digging son of a bitch," the kid yelped and went for his gun.

Slyke had the revolver out before the kid cleared leather. Even in his drunken state, the kid could see the .44 hole of Slyke's gun lined up with his head. A sly smile spread on his face and he turned slightly to replace his revolver.

Slyke put the gun back in his holster and said, "Now find some place to sleep."

"Sure, mister, sure," the kid said, his voice suddenly anxious to please. "I'll find a place."

"That's good then," Slyke said and watched as the kid got back to his feet and headed toward the door.

He was halfway to the door, feeling like a whipped pup, when he remembered what Carter had told him, about a bullet in the back making a man just as dead as one in the chest. Whirling on his heels, he turned back to the miner as he went for the gun.

Slyke caught a glimpse of motion in the bar's mirror and turned, gun already out. The kid never had a chance. Slyke fired twice, two .44 slugs pounding into the kid's chest. The first set him a step back; the second brought him to his knees as the gun fell from his grasp.

"Lordy, I'm just bleeding all over," the kid moaned as the blood began to pour from the wounds. Lifting a shaking hand, he tried to plug one of the bullet holes with a finger. Then he fell over dead, a finger sunk to the first knuckle in an open chest wound. He did not know that he had finally gotten his fondest wish. At last, he was just like Carter.

Chapter 12

Jessie and the sheriff were eating stew and stale bread, Jessie trying to get the fatty meat down and the sheriff trying to figure out what to do with her.

When the shots came in quick succession, the sheriff tumbled the stew across his lap and ran for the office door. "Just stay put here, lady," he shouted as he reached the door and vanished into the street. But Jessie was right behind him, instinctively reaching for the Colt with peachwood grips, which she no longer had.

When they entered the saloon, the sheriff found Slyke, somberly drinking alone at a table, and the dead boy sprawled on the floor, a checkered tablecloth covering him to the waist.

"That dead one, he started it, Sheriff," the bardog said anxiously. "Took off on Slyke until there wasn't a choice."

"Tried to back-shoot him," someone else put in, followed by maybe a half dozen yeps and that's rights.

"Okay, okay," the sheriff said, kneeling close to the body. "Let's see what we have here." Then he pulled the cloth off.

103

The sheriff studied the face for a long time, shaking his head. "Anybody know this fella?" he asked.

Jessie stepped farther into the room. "That's one of them, Sheriff!" she screamed.

"One of who?" he asked, turning his head around to look at her.

"One of the men who abducted me!" Jessie answered, pointing. "That's definitely one of them!"

The sheriff pulled the cloth slowly back up over the dead boy's face and stood up. "Lady, is there any dead person in this town who *didn't* try to abduct you?"

"Sheriff, I tell you that's one of them," Jessie insisted.

Slyke walked over then and the sheriff said, "Look, she ain't right in the head, I don't think."

"All the rest of her looks mighty fine, though," someone in the back of the room said. And even Slyke's hard looks could not silence the laughter.

"Quit, you pack of hyenas!" the sheriff shouted. "Case any of you forget, there's a dead man laying out here! Let's have a little respect, such as you know how to show. Now I got official law business to tend to here."

The room quieted.

The sheriff looked around the half-filled saloon, waiting for the silence to soak in. "Now, I'm conducting an official sheriff's inquest and inquiry here," he said loudly. "You are all under oath. Do you all understand that?"

Half the room nodded in sure agreement. The other half shuffled nervously, not exactly certain what direction the lawman's line of questioning would take.

The sheriff waited a little longer, then said, "Was this here a fair and decent fight?"

"It was fair, Sheriff," the bartender said. "Boy tried to shoot Slyke in the back, and Slyke got the better of him."

"Anybody got anything different to say?" the sheriff asked.

Nobody said anything further.

"All right then, that officially concludes the inquiry," the sheriff announced. "Somebody find the undertaker and arrange for burial."

They were halfway across the darkened street before Jessie caught up with the sheriff. "That man, that dead man in there, was one of the train robbers," she said. "If you don't believe me, then perhaps the railroad officials will."

Slyke was moving up on them in a slow trot.

"Now what in hell do you want?" the lawman asked, annoyed, as Slyke came up on the other side of him. "Ain't you got enough trouble for one night?"

"Need to talk to the lady here," Slyke said.

"Then maybe you figure that you don't have enough trouble," the lawman answered and picked up his pace to be rid of the two.

Jessie stopped in her tracks and stared at Slyke. She saw that he might have been a bastard, devious as hell, but he sure was a handsome one. "And would you like to call my sanity into question, too?" she asked.

"Hell, I just wanted to talk to you is all," Slyke said. She could smell the whiskey on his breath. "What are you going to do now that everyone thinks you're crazy and all?"

She thought for a second before answering. "I'm going to find Ki, then get in touch with Ames again and find out exactly what is going on."

"Gonna be tough, without any money and all," Slyke said.

"And just what would you propose, Mr. Slyke?" she asked, hands on hips, staring at him defiantly.

"How 'bout you and me get a room and a bottle?" he said. "Tomorrow, I'll give you enough to get on to Gold Hill."

The blow came so fast, he didn't see it. But he felt it sure enough, the palm of her hand connecting with his jaw solidly. The strength of it sent his head snapping to one side. Then she hit him again, this time kicking out with her boot, bringing it up between his legs. The pain exploded in his groin and shot up through his insides, knocking him to the ground. Behind him the saloon's batwings were crowded with laughing men and a few women.

"Now, what was that for?" he asked, rolling to his side, one hand wedged between his legs against the pain.

"The first was for not believing me," Jessie said, standing over him, legs slightly apart. "The second was for thinking I'm some whore you can take for the price of a bottle of whiskey and a coach ticket."

"Hell, I didn't mean nothing by it," Slyke said, getting painfully to his knees. "Nothing at all."

"Well, I did," Jessie said, then turned heel and walked into the sheriff's office.

As she entered, Jessie heard a few of the onlookers shouting, but they were quickly silenced, no doubt by some unheard threat of Slyke's.

"I thought I saw the last of you," the sheriff said, turning the lamp up. "Now what do you want?"

"Need a place to stay," Jessie conceded. "Just for the night. After that, I'll be out of your way."

Removing his hat, the sheriff ran a hand through his hair. "All right, you can stay here," he said at last. "Sleep in the cell next to those two."

"Why not just put her in here with us?" one of the men called.

"It ain't bad," the sheriff said as Jessie eyed the cell suspiciously. "Hell, I've slept in there plenty of times. Not too bad."

Jessie watched the men in the next cell, then let her eyes wander over to the empty cage—a small wooden cot with a thin mattress and a thick wool blanket. She had slept in worse places. "I guess I don't have much of a choice," she said at last.

"None at all," the sheriff answered. "I'll leave the door open for you. Be back at seven in the morning. Don't talk to those two and you'll be fine."

The sheriff was no sooner out the door when the two prisoners began calling her. "Hey, lady, you ever bed a dead man?" the tall one called in a whisper. "We're dead men in here. They gonna hang us up in Gold Hill."

Jessie didn't answer.

"Sure would be nice to do it, just once more 'fore we died," the other said. "Sure nice. No sense sending a man on without giving him a taste of what he'll be missing forever."

Jessie stretched out on the cot, not bothering to take her boots off.

"Would be nice, Miss Starbuck," the tall one said. "Just once more."

Jessie opened her eyes, but did not turn. It was the first time in a long while anybody had called her by her name.

"I know who you are, Miss Starbuck," the short one called. "Seen your picture in a San Antone paper like," he said. "Seen you was buying something or other. Daughter of Alex Starbuck."

Jessie brought her feet off the cot and stared across the darkness to where the men stood against the bars.

"So, you'll tell the sheriff?" she asked.

"That depends on how nice you are to us," the little one said. "Depends on how fine our last earthly pleasures are. If you get my drift?"

"I get it," she answered and lay back down on the bed.

She was almost asleep when the tall one called, "That fella that died, one they had propped up here, remember him?"

"The one you murdered, you mean?" she asked, talking up to the ceiling.

"Let's just say he died," the short one said.

"I'd say that someone crushed his skull and then cut his throat," Jessie answered. "Made a mess of his face, too."

"What if we just said he was a careless sort?" the small one tried. "Say he met with an unfortunate accident like."

"Then I'd say you were lying," Jessie shot back. "Now, I'm going to sleep."

"What if I said we knew who he was working for?" the tall one said smugly. "He laid out the whole plan. Mentioned your name quite a bit."

Jessie brought her legs off the side of the bed again and stared into the next cell. Both men were grinning wide. "What'd he say?" she asked.

"I thought we was liars?" the short one said. "Not good enough to talk to the likes of you."

"What did he say?" Jessie insisted, coming closer, but still keeping a safe distance.

"What you going to show us?" the tall one asked.

Jessie put on a smile and fumbled with the top button of her shirt. "Whatever you want to see."

"That's a start now," the tall one said.

"I got something better," she said, undoing the button. "You give me proof that you know Carter was the one who robbed the train, you might get a reward, not a rope."

"He had a pocket full of money," the short one said. "Spending it, too. But he spent it all before we met him."

"Who was he working for?" Jessie asked, stepping closer and undoing another button.

"He was working for Jonathan Ames, up in Gold Hill," the short one said. "Told us the whole plan. Asked if we wanted in on it."

The news struck Jessie like a blow. "What was the plan?" she asked, taking another step forward.

It was one step too close, and she knew it as soon as her foot came down. The tall one's hand shot out between the bars and grabbed her by the belt, just next to the buckle. She struggled briefly, then he pulled to him, bringing her right up against the bars so that his leering face was inches from her own.

But she recovered quickly. Sending both her hands between the bars, she grabbed the man by the back of his head and pulled, smashing his head into a crossbar and opening a large, bloody wound at his hairline. When she yanked him forward again, the dazed man showed little fight and his head came skinning through between the rough iron bars.

The little one was reaching around, trying to get at Jessie. When he couldn't, he tried to pull his now-panicked friend free by his waist. That's when their legs became tangled and the tall one tripped. The sound of his neck snapping was like dried wood and was followed by a hollow grunt. He stood there, held up by the crossbar, shuddering for a second, before the life faded from his eyes.

"You killed him!" the little one said. "Damn, you killed him!" Then he started wailing for the sheriff.

The lawman had quarters above the jail and office. Jessie could hear his footsteps echoing across the floor above and down the stairs behind. He ran in from the back, partially dressed and fully furious. It took him about two seconds to size up the situation. "Now, why'd I know that it had to do with you?" he said, giving Jessie a cold stare that lasted no less than a full half minute. "How'd I know that?"

★

Chapter 13

Ki awakened the sleeping Dorry before dawn. She hadn't opened her eyes when her two arms encircled his neck and drew him down to her. "Oh, you want to do it again," she purred sleepily, her eyes coming open just a bit.

"We must leave," Ki answered, lifting himself from her grasp. "We must leave now."

"But we have time, don't we?" she asked, sitting up now. "Just for a little while."

"No, we must find Jessie," he said resolutely and stood up.

She pouted for only a moment, then got to her feet.

"Well, we have time to eat something, don't we?" she asked.

"I have some food," Ki answered. "We can eat in the saddle."

If this news didn't sit well with her, Dorry didn't show it. Almost immediately she began to roll the blankets while Ki saddled the horses. Soon they were leading their animals down the gentle incline toward the main trail. Dawn was just breaking, gray and blue in the sky.

Ki heard them before Dorry—riders moving quickly along the trail. He raised his hand for her to stop. Listening closely, he counted horses. Five in all, and moving fast.

"What? Someone's coming?" she asked.

"Many someones," Ki answered, then shushed her into silence. From the darkness of the trees, Ki peered out onto the trail as they passed. Yes, many riders. Five in all and heading for town. They did not look like ranchers or miners. Their horses, although weary from the night ride, were expensive. So were the men's clothes. Mail-order suits and range outfits that had never seen a full day's work.

Dorry, kneeling beside Ki, brought her breath in sharply at the sight.

"You know those men?" Ki asked after they had passed.

"That big one, the one closest to us, his name is D. G. Quimby," she said. "Mean, real mean."

Ki rose slowly, pulling himself up with the staff, as the riders passed out of sight. "What is his profession?"

"Don't make much difference to him. Anything on the other side of the law," Dorry answered. "But I heard he wears a badge."

"He is a sheriff?"

"Deputy is more like it," she said. "Moves into town and scares the sheriff or buys the badge from a judge. Then deputizes his men. But it don't mean nothing. Man he works for, rancher or whatnot, is the one that pays him. The one he answers to."

"He is a regulator, then?" Ki asked.

"Call it whatever you want, but I never heard of him bringing in anyone alive for a judge," Dorry said bitterly. "And I heard he's brought in enough men tied over the saddle. Call him a regulator or bounty hunter, if that's what you want, but he's a drygulcher. It's born into him, they say."

"Who does he work for?"

"Whoever has the most money," Dorry said. "Doesn't matter. Only thing he's particular about is getting paid."

"We must leave then," Ki answered as he began to walk. "I have a bad feeling about Mr. Quimby."

"Well, you wouldn't be the first," Dorry said as she followed him down the trail.

They hadn't gone two miles, following in the fresh tracks of Quimby and his men, before Dorry asked Ki, "You ever think about marrying? Settling down like?"

"I have thought of it," Ki answered, feeling a small knot of dread rising in his stomach. It was not the first time he'd been asked that question. Yet he did not know how to answer. He was fond of Dorry.

"I thought 'bout it," she said. "Lotta times."

Ki did not answer. There was no answer in words to this sort of questioning. Only action, turning the reins and riding to the closest preacher, would do.

"Thought 'bout what it would be like, having a little house," she said. "Kids. A man that worked at something full-time. It would be different."

"Different than what?" Ki asked.

"Than having six, eight men a night pawing at you," she said. "It gets uh . . ."

Ki could not imagine what she felt, so he kept quiet as she thought of the word.

"Boring," she said at last, with a note of small triumph in her voice. "Boring, exactly."

They rode past noon, stopping only to rest and water the horses twice. Ki had been reading the trail carefully, and what he saw disturbed him. Those men, Quimby and the others, were getting farther and farther ahead. Their horses would not be good for much when they reached town, but Ki figured that men like that cared little for horses. Men like that cared for little at all, except maybe money.

The sheriff returned in late afternoon from the railhead, where he had shipped one live prisoner off for trial. The dead one had been buried that morning, along with the boy that Slyke had killed. As he rode back into town on the buckboard, the sheriff thought up a plan for dealing with the crazy lady. Come tomorrow, he would give her enough money for a coach to Gold Hill. That was a big enough town where they wouldn't notice one more crazy person. Hell, Gold Hill was probably big enough so that they'd welcome her with a brass band and speeches.

As the sheriff stepped down from the wagon, Jessie came out of his office to meet him. He was maybe twenty feet from her when she said, "Well, you've got a nerve, you bastard."

He was about to answer her, saying something about how he was only coming back to his office, when a voice spoke up behind him. "I'm sorry, it was a damn wrong thing to say."

The sheriff turned and saw Slyke, standing there with his hat in his hand, looking the worse for a night of drinking and killing.

"You're damn right it was the wrong thing to say," Jessie answered, looking right past the sheriff, who sidestepped around her and into the office.

"I just wanted to apologize and to buy you supper," Slyke said.

Jessie saw immediately that Slyke genuinely was sorry, but she couldn't figure if he was sorry for insulting her or sorry for drinking as much as he had.

"Heard about what happened, last night," Slyke said. Then a small, amused smile broke over his face.

"Suppose I should be grateful for getting off so easy."

It was the smile that did it for her. So genuine and sincere, and boyish, she couldn't resist. "Ham steak and eggs with coffee sounds right," she said at last.

Slyke smiled again, wider. "Sounds right to me, too," he said, putting his hat back on.

They were crossing the street together when they saw the horsemen. There were five of them, their horses weary and wild-eyed from a long ride. They entered town at a walk, five across blocking the entire street.

It was Slyke who slowed his pace, bringing Jessie alongside him as the horsemen approached. "Sons of bitches," he mumbled under his breath as they drew nearer.

When they were close enough, the one in the middle of the line grinned and nodded to Slyke and Jessie. "You're blocking the street, Slyke," he said pleasantly. Then to Jessie, "Ma'am."

Slyke turned, as if just noticing them. Except for the one in the middle, the fat one, all were lean, hard-looking men. They leaned slightly forward in their saddles, hands resting on guns.

Slyke nodded without smiling, then said one word, "Quimby."

"Here on official business," the fat man said, then opened his coat to show off the tarnished tin star that hung on its inside. "Official law business," he added.

"Then we best let you be at it," Slyke said and started walking again, Jessie alongside him.

They were well past the men and on the boards before the horses started moving again. When they did, they formed a line directly for the post outside the sheriff's office.

"Who were those men?" Jessie asked, as they entered the cafe.

"D. G. Quimby," Slyke said, taking a seat at one of the tables. "And his so-called deputies."

"He's a lawman?" Jessie asked.

"Deputy," Slyke answered. "But that don't mean much. He never brought a man in legally that didn't have a price on his head, and probably shot a few 'cause some mining company owner or big-money rancher thought it would be convenientlike to have him do it."

"What's he doing here?" Jessie asked.

"Probably investigating that train robbery you say you were at," Slyke answered. "Working for the Starbucks or the railroad."

"He's not working for me," Jessie said firmly.

Across the table, Slyke made a kind of pained face that showed he still didn't believe that she was Jessie Starbuck. "Don't matter," he said softly.

"It matters because you still don't believe me," Jessie answered, her cheeks flushing red.

"If I did believe you, if I thought you were a Starbuck, for an instant, I wouldn't be sitting down to eat with you," Slyke said.

"Oh, and why is that?" Jessie asked. "You too good for a Starbuck?"

"Damn right," Slyke said. "I'm particular about who I eat with, drink with, and go to bed with. Starbucks the ones that want to bring in that new hydraulic system. Tear the hell out of everything. That's only what I can prove—"

Jessie was about to interrupt, when the sheriff did it for her. "Slyke," the lawman said. "I'm sorry as hell, but I got someone over at the office wants to talk to you and your lady friend here."

Slyke stiffened at the table, then turned slowly on the sheriff. "Quimby?" he asked.

The lawman nodded slowly.

"Tell that fat son of a bitch he knows where to find me," Slyke said. "I ain't crossing the street to see him."

"Now, don't be like that," the sheriff urged gently. "I don't want no trouble. None at all."

"Then run that bastard and his men out of town," Slyke suggested.

"I ain't gonna get into it with you here and now," the sheriff said. "You go see him or he's gonna see you. Don't make a bunch of difference either way."

"We're eating," Slyke said, turning toward Jessie.

★

Chapter 14

Jessie and Slyke ate their meal in peace. Though Jessie didn't enjoy her plate much, all the time expecting the sheriff to return or, worse, the five men to come through the door. Slyke, too, was anxious, not talking as he cut into his meat, then forked it into his mouth.

As they were finishing their coffee, Jessie looked up and saw Slyke's crinkled brow across the table. "You ever get that room?" she asked. "The one at the hotel."

Slyke nodded, his face grim.

"That's good," she said.

"Why's that good?" Slyke asked, his eyes locked on the cafe's window and the street beyond.

"Because, then all we need is the bottle of whiskey," she said with a slight smile that nonetheless conveyed exactly what she was plotting.

"You know, I was thinking about giving up drinking," he said, smiling back as his eyes lowered to hers.

"Oh, since when?" she asked.

"Since I woke up this morning with a pain that would kill two men," he said. "And a mouth that tasted like a saddle blanket."

"Head hurts, stomach sour, and kinda sick feeling?"

"Yep."

Jessie smiled wider. "You know, I have just the cure," she said.

The small room could have passed easily for a large closet, as it was barely big enough for the bed. Slyke turned to shut the door, and when he faced Jessie again, she was unfastening her shirt.

"Easy there," he said. "What's the rush?"

She came to him in one step, and he kissed her deeply, feeling her full breasts crush against his chest. They were still locked in each other's arms as they lowered themselves backward across the narrow bed.

"You know, I am awful sorry about last night," she whispered as he finished the job of unbuttoning her shirt.

"How sorry?" he asked, teasing, a finger tracing a fine line between her breasts.

"Oh, very sorry," she replied, teasing back. "I'll show you just how sorry if you let me."

Slyke eased the soft cotton garment off her shoulders. "You know, I'm more than a little sorry, too. There wasn't any call for acting like that. None."

"Will you prove it to me?" Jessie asked, her breath coming a little short as he worked a patient finger over her left nipple.

"I'd like to try," Slyke answered. Then, dipping his head to her, he kissed first one breast, then the other.

Jessie arched her back, offering up her full breasts to him. Cupping one of them gently in his large hand, he began kissing it, first on the side, then softly, slowly, toward the center. Soon his tongue was teasing and playing across the nipple, exciting it to hardness.

"Oh, that feels so good," Jessie moaned, as she leaned back. "So very good."

In answer, he took the rigid nipple in his mouth and held it gently between his lips, pulling at it just the smallest bit. When he had finished with one breast, he began working on the other. But it was pleasant work indeed.

Jessie slipped her arms from the shirt and closed her eyes completely. Soon, she was working a hand down between Slyke's legs, seeking out the hardened bulge beneath the rough canvas of his trousers. She stroked him for a long time, teasing with her fingers, then using the palm of her hand to press and massage gently. When she judged he'd had enough teasing, she let her fingers work their way upward, where she found the thick brass of his gunbelt, and the smaller buckle of his trousers belt.

She unfastened both deftly, and Slyke rolled onto her, abandoning the gunbelt at the side of the bed as he positioned himself between her legs and continued to work on her breasts, neck, and shoulders, showering them with small, gentle kisses.

Truly amazing, Jessie thought, that such gentleness could come from such a large man. And a man that was so deadly proficient with a gun.

Soon she was working on the buttons of his trousers, arching slightly forward to work her fingers between them. When she finally managed to wedge her hand inside, his swollen manhood filled her palm with a throbbing warmth.

Working her hand lower, he arched his hips upward, and she let her fingertips play along the underside.

Slyke moaned and she continued. Then the moan turned into a small groan of pain. "Still a little tender from last night," he said, as if apologizing.

Jessie brought her hand up a little and traced a thin line with one finger from the base to the top, along the underside of his swollen manhood.

121

Then they were undressing, their hands flying to disrobe each other. In seconds, their clothes lay tangled across the bed.

Jessie eased Slyke down onto his back and straddled him. Slowly, using one hand, she guided him up inside her as she lowered herself on his member. Her wetness engulfed him completely. She squirmed slightly as she took the entire shaft up inside her; then, very deliberately, she began to rock, first forward, then back. The slick shaft slid partially out, then back in again.

Reaching up, Slyke took both her breasts in his hands, letting the hard nipples jab his palms. Jessie rose, and the breasts rubbed pleasingly against his hands. Soon she was moving faster and faster, raising and lowering herself, her hands resting at the top of his thighs.

Slyke met every motion as he raised and lowered himself off the bed with a thrusting that set the old, rusting springs into singing.

When the motion became too intense, Slyke let his hands fall from Jessie's breasts and steadied her with a firm grip on her hips. Her breasts, free of his gentle grasp, flew up and down with each motion. Then, very slyly, she reached down and behind her and began running gentle fingers teasingly over his balls, the pain long-forgotten as the teasing increased.

Jessie felt the intense pleasure building, beginning deep inside her and spreading out in warm spasms across her legs and up her breasts. Deep in her moistness she began grabbing, as if trying to pull him deeper into her.

A loud scream rose in Jessie's throat, and she bit her lip to suppress it. With one final upward thrust, Slyke exploded deep within, filling her with warmth as the spasms of pleasure subsided.

When they were finished, Jessie leaned forward and Slyke took first one nipple, then the other in his mouth, caressing each one in turn with his knowing tongue.

They slept for a long time, tangled together in a bed littered with clothes and sheets. When Jessie awoke, reluctantly opening her eyes from the warm glow of sleep, it was dark beyond the paper screen of the window.

"Slyke," she whispered, bringing her mouth close to his ear.

He grunted sleepily, but did not attempt to roll over.

"Wake up, darling, it's dark," she said, letting two fingers stroke the hair above his ear.

He came slowly awake, opening his eyes to her face hovering closely over him. A slow smile spread across his lips. It was a smile from the memory of the afternoon, and a smile that bespoke his gladness that she was still there in bed with him.

He turned his face away from Jessie and studied the window for only a moment before turning back. "Too late to ride tonight," he said.

"Yes," she answered, letting a finger twirl and explore in the soft hairs of his beard.

"Maybe pay for another night," he offered. "Set off tomorrow."

"Yes, that would be nice," she answered dreamily.

They heard the footsteps at the same time. Slyke silenced Jessie with a finger to her lips before she could say anything more. Listening, she made out two sets of boots, moving slowly down the hall toward them.

The footsteps stopped just outside the door as Slyke reached slowly over the edge of the bed and pulled the Colt from its holster.

Then there was a timid knock at the door. Too timid for a man. Slyke nodded to Jessie, and she said, "Yes?"

A second later the door burst open. Slyke pushed Jessie hard, sending her to the floor as he fired at the outline of a man. The shot hit the figure high on the shoulder, and a shotgun exploded in the darkened room, sending its pellets straight up into the rough ceiling.

Jessie spun, bringing the heel of her foot crashing into the man's kneecap as the shotgun went off again, this time tearing through the paper window shade and shattering the glass.

The man went down, falling back into his companion, as a second shot from Slyke's revolver caught him in the chest.

Jessie lunged, twisting the shotgun from the dying man's hands and thrusting it upward, barrel-first, into the gut of the second. The twin 12-gauge barrels hit hard, but had little effect. Another shot thundered from the room, and the wooden door frame splintered, sending the second attacker retreating into the hall as the dead man crumpled on top of Jessie.

In a flash of movement, Slyke was out of bed and leaping, stark naked, over Jessie and the dead man. Out in the hall, two more shots sounded, and then there was the sound of running feet, booted and bare-foot, on the stairs.

Jessie pulled herself up and retreated back into the room for a blanket. Then she was out the door. She'd taken two steps when she heard the sound of a gun cocking. "Hold it right there, miss," Quimby said.

She froze in place.

"Hands up," Quimby said, moving closer.

"You think I've a weapon under here?" she asked.

"I'm gonna find out now, ain't I?" Quimby said. "Put them hands up."

Jessie raised her hands, releasing her hold on the blanket. The rough wool square fell to the floor, leaving her naked.

Behind her Quimby let out a low whistle of crude appreciation at the sight.

"Enjoying yourself?" Jessie asked sarcastically.

"Man's greatest blessing is enjoying his work," Quimby answered. "Now turn round."

Jessie turned, more mad than embarrassed at having to display her body for Quimby. The man was a pig and took no pains to conceal it. Perhaps he even took a perverse pride in his own piggishness.

He took his time in looking at her. Even in the dim hall, lit by only a single lamp, his eyes feasted from head to foot, then back again.

"Have you satisfied yourself that I'm quite unarmed, Mr. Quimby?" she asked.

"You are some woman," Quimby sighed. "Okay, make yourself decent. We're going visiting."

To his continuing discredit, Quimby stood in the doorway, feet straddling the dead man, gun lazy in his hand, and watched her dress. When she had just pulled her boots on, Slyke appeared, though not naked. He was wearing an oilskin duster, no doubt scrounged up by the manager. Behind him was the sheriff, looking nervous as hell.

"Now, you gonna tell me that dead man there tried abducting you, too?" the sheriff asked, nodding to the corpse in the doorway.

Jessie ignored the question and Quimby ignored the sheriff, instead addressing Slyke. "Fine-looking woman you bedded yourself there, Slyke. Real fine."

Even in the oilskin, Slyke was fast. His fist snaked out and caught Quimby on the jaw, knocking his head back against the bullet-ravaged door frame. He was bringing the gun up when Slyke caught him again, this time in his gut. The blow doubled him over, and Slyke took the gun.

"That's enough of that," the lawman said. "Slyke, you're way out of line here. Quimby's a duly deputized officer of the law. So was his man, there."

"A drunk sheriff don't make a man the law by pinning a badge on him," Slyke said. "And neither does that twenty dollars a month you earn saying you are."

"Don't make me do it," the sheriff said. "Don't make me shoot you. Now, give me his gun. And while you're at it, hand over that one in your pocket, too."

"What's going on here, Sheriff?" Jessie asked.

"Mr. Quimby here has a duly sworn warrant for your arrest," the sheriff said.

"Damn right, you she-devil," Quimby gasped, as he straightened up a little. "Duly sworn and stamped. Seems we're going to be doing some traveling together. That please you?"

"What's the charge, Sheriff?" Slyke asked.

"Fraud," the sheriff said. "She's been going around saying she's that dead Starbuck woman. Seems the dead woman's partner didn't take too kindly to it."

It fell into place then for Jessie. The dead man in the jail hadn't been lying about Ames being in on it with Carter. Mr. Jonathan Ames, drinker of fine French wines and devoted patron of opera, had sent Carter after her on the train, and now he had sent this Quimby bastard.

"That ain't against the law, being crazy," Slyke said. "If it were, half of Gold Hill and San Francisco would be in jail."

"Against the law sending telegrams asking for money, and blackmailing," Quimby said. "Mr. Ames got a

126

stack of 'em back in Gold Hill. You think this is the first town she's tried this in? We just never caught up to her till now."

Jessie recoiled at the lie. "This is ridiculous. I can clear it up now, if you'd let me wire San Francisco."

"See there, she's still at it," Quimby said, pointing an accusing finger in Jessie's direction.

"Well, I just don't know," the sheriff said with a slow shake of his head. "I just don't know."

"That's fine, Sheriff," Quimby offered agreeably. "Just lock her up for the night. Mr. Ames is coming in tomorrow on the stage. He'll clear it up for you."

"Sheriff, you don't understand, Ames wants to kill me," Jessie said. "Don't you see, that's why he's sent this bastard out. To kill me."

Slyke shrugged slightly, not knowing what to say.

"Now you're telling me this Mr. Ames is after you," the sheriff said. "First it was the dead fella in the jail. Then the boy Slyke here shot. Then Mr. Quimby here. Now Mr. Ames is after you."

Jessie saw the futility of it, but answered anyway. "That's right," she said. "They're all working together."

The sheriff's grim eyes went from Jessie to Quimby and then to Slyke, who shrugged again. "I reckon it won't be nothing to lock her up until Mr. Ames comes in," he said. "Then maybe we can straighten this thing out."

★

Chapter 15

Ten miles outside of town and an hour away from full dark, Dorry's horse turned up lame. It was hard to tell at first whether the horse was in genuine pain or just finally relenting under the weight of a lifetime of hard luck and bad trails.

Then Ki watched it as it brought the pressure off its left front hoof for a quarter mile. He knew then that the horse would not make it to town. The animal's sad, red-rimmed eyes stared out in a kind of final sorrow as it continued to limp along.

Dorry came down off the saddle as Ki bent to examine the horse. One look at the animal told him that somewhere behind them, in a livery, someone was having a good laugh over selling a whore such a bad animal. The hoof was split many times, the wounds were old and new, the older ones not healed properly. Someone had painted the scarred tissue over with varnish to disguise the damage. But now, on the second day on the trail, the varnish was all worn off. It was only through some stroke of large luck or the determination of the damned that the beast had held out this long. Now it was bleeding, nearly coming apart under the weight of Dorry and her bags.

"Is it bad?" Dorry asked, concerned as she bent down to stare over Ki's shoulder.

"Yes, very bad," Ki answered, patting the fetlock gently, then letting the hoof fall from his hands. "Horse must be destroyed."

"Destroyed, you mean like shot?" Dorry asked, horrified at the notion at killing the animal that had carried her away from the joy-house.

"Yes, shot," Ki answered.

"Well, you're not shooting my horse," she said indignantly. "Not that horse. Shoot any damn horse you want, but you ain't shooting this one."

"I cannot shoot the horse," Ki answered.

"Damn right you can't," she said with a note of triumph.

"I cannot shoot the horse because I have no gun," Ki said. "Must use knife. Very quick."

Dorry's face turned to a mask of determination that was clear even in the dim light. "The hell you will!"

"It must be destroyed," Ki said. "It is very old and in pain. I promise to be very quick. It will feel little."

Dorry came forward and examined the hoof for herself. Even to her untrained eye, the damage was obvious. "Okay, then," she said. "We'll kill it. But not here and not with a knife. You have to do it proper."

"Proper?"

"Yes, in town," Dorry said, with her hands on her hips and her eyes squinting defiance. "You can shoot it in town."

Ki saw that it was useless to argue with her. Rather, he began to untie her bags from the animal in order to lighten its load. Perhaps, with no one riding and no bags to carry, it would make it the few more miles to town.

But no sooner had Ki pulled the battered bags off the

130

beast, than Dorry grabbed one and disappeared into the trees with it.

"Where are you going?" Ki called as she vanished into the darkness just off the road.

"I have to change my clothes," she called back. "I can't ride into town looking like this. I won't have folks seeing me done up like some damn saddle tramp."

A few minutes later, as Ki was securing the bags to his horse, she reemerged from the trees. She was carrying a small brass hurricane lamp with a fancy reflector of engraved brass and a pink glass well. "Do you have a match?" she asked.

Wordlessly, Ki handed her a match. She struck it on the heel of her shoe and lit the lamp. In the yellow kerosene light, Ki could see that she had dressed in her finest. But her finest was faded purple silk and a small, crumpled hat.

"Just 'cause we ain't stepping off a stage doesn't mean I can't look like maybe I did," she said, her face heavy with powder and her cheeks painted.

"And the lamp?" Ki asked, knowing better than to argue a woman's appearance with her. But to his eye, she looked better without the powder or red cheeks.

"To see where we're stepping, of course," she said. "For the horse."

"Of course," Ki answered, knowing that to argue this point would also prove a fruitless endeavor.

And that's how they proceeded, Dorry sitting very ladylike, sidesaddle across Ki's mount, the reins of her animal tied to the pommel, while Ki walked in front, staff in one hand, reins and lighted lamp in the other.

Slyke watched sadly as they closed the barred door behind Jessie. "Find Ki," she said, through the bars. "Telegraph Texas."

131

Quimby was grinning broadly at the sight.

"You're doing the right thing here, Sheriff," Quimby said. "Mr. Ames, he doesn't forget his friends."

"I hope so," the sheriff answered, leading the two men through the front door, out on the boards. Then to Slyke, "You staying in town?"

"I've seen enough," Slyke answered. "I'm riding back now."

"That's good thinking there, Slyke," Quimby said. "Head on back to your pans."

"I've seen enough of you, too, Quimby," Slyke answered.

It was Quimby and his remaining two men who called and waved Slyke off as he headed his buckboard out of town. On his worst days, he wouldn't have stood for them. Not at all. But this was worse than his worst day, and he needed some time to sort things out.

Slyke wasn't five miles out of town on the wide trail when he saw the light. It was just like a splash of dull yellow in the distance on a straight stretch of trail. Then, as he rode closer, he saw it bob gently at the center of the road.

"Now, what in hell is this?" he said to himself, resting a hand on his pistol. He'd had enough surprises, most of them unpleasant, in the last two days. He wasn't looking for any more.

As the light came closer, he saw that there was a Chinaman holding it. The Chinaman was walking in front of a horse, holding a fancy wall lamp and a broom handle.

"Now, what in hell . . . ," Slyke mumbled again.

And then he saw the other horse. When they were close enough, he saw the entire scene. There was a Chinaman with a lamp and a broom or hoe handle, leading a horse with a whore and a bunch of leather

132

satchels tied to it. The other horse was limping bad. Slyke felt his jaw drop open as the three of them met in the center of the trail, coming to a stop in the small pool of light cast by the lamp.

The Chinese fellow raised the broom handle in greeting, then very distinctly said, "Hello."

"Hello," Slyke murmured, then closed his jaw through some act of will.

"Good evening," the woman in the purplish dress said. "How far to town?"

"Few miles," Slyke managed to answer. His voice sounded strangely hollow to his ears.

"Thank you," the Chinese man said.

"Very most 'preciated," the woman added, then adjusted her hat.

Slyke watched as they began to move again, carefully turning to the side of the road to avoid his buckboard.

When they were nearly even with Slyke, they stopped again. "Please, be so kind as to tell us, if Miss Jessica Starbuck is in this town," the man said. "We were unfortunately separated during the train robbery a few days ago. Perhaps you have heard of it?"

"I think I might have heard something 'bout it," Slyke answered. It was then that he thought to himself, Just keep moving and put all this craziness behind. But instead of snapping the reins to the horse, he said, "Excuse me for asking, but your name is Ki, ain't it?"

Now it was the Chinese fellow's turn to be surprised. "Yes, it is," he said. "But how . . ."

"Well, Mr. Ki," Slyke answered. "I think we better have ourselves a little talk."

★

Chapter 16

Jessie had spent a sleepless night in the jail. She watched morosely as the sky turned from black and moonless to gray. When it was a little after dawn, the sheriff came in with a platter of eggs and corn bread. He unlocked the door, slid the plate on the floor, then turned to build a fire in the small stove, for coffee.

"Sheriff, you can't let them take me today," she called from the cell. "If I ride out with them, I won't reach Gold Hill."

"I don't know what you're so worked up about," he said without turning from the stove. "That so-called business partner of yours is due in on the stage today. If you are who you say, he'll clear it up."

Even though she saw the futility of it, she tried anyway. "Ames is the one behind all this," she said. "I don't know why, but he's the one."

"Lady, just try to see it from where I'm standing," the sheriff said. "You come in here with some cock 'n' bull story about being a rich Texas lady, then point a finger at every dead man in town that he was trying to abduct you, while performing married acts with

Mr. Slyke. Now, you tell me what you would like me to do?"

"I'd like for you to believe me, for one," Jessie answered.

The sheriff was about to say something when the boy from the telegraph office appeared in the door. He was holding a slip of paper.

"Now, what do you want?" the sheriff said, turning to the boy.

"Telegraph, just came over the wire," the youth said.

The sheriff took the sheet of paper and read it carefully, his lips moving only slightly. "Says that business has delayed Mr. Jonathan Ames. He's gonna meet up with you when you get where you're going."

"Sheriff, if you send me off with those men, I won't reach Gold Hill and it'll be on your head," Jessie said.

"I think I can live with that," the sheriff answered. Then to the boy, "Take this on over to the hotel and show it to Quimby."

The boy returned only a blank look to the sheriff's request.

"Quimby?" the lad asked.

"Oh, hell, boy, I'll do it," the sheriff said, grabbed the slip of paper from the boy, and stormed out of the room.

Left suddenly alone in the room, the youth looked over at Jessie, his eyes sort of glazed over. Finally he asked, "It true what they're saying about you?"

"What are they saying?" Jessie asked, moving toward the bars.

"That you're gonna jail," the lad answered. "Maybe even hang. That you caused a racket and fuss over at the hotel with Mr. Slyke."

136

"That's what they're saying, is it?" Jessie answered.

"Yes, ma'am," the lad said. "Ladies are saying you're no better than a Gold Hill whore. But the whores, they saying you no better than nothing, 'cause on account you giving it away for free."

Jessie, disgusted, said, "If that's what they're saying, then I guess it's true, isn't it?"

"You really give it away?"

It was in the hopeful way that the lad asked it and in his eager face that Jessie saw her chance. "To those I like," she said. "And to the cute ones."

The lad took a step closer. "You think I'm cute?"

She cocked her head to one side, as if seriously considering it. The lad was sallow, his face marked with deep scars, and his hair so oily it should have slid off his head. "You got something about you," she said at last. "Too bad we can't do anything about it."

The lad's face sunk with disappointment. "Oh, I guess not," he mumbled.

"Unless you get those keys off the sheriff's desk," Jessie said. "He won't be back for a spell."

"I couldn't do that," the boy said.

"And I can't do nothing in here," Jessie said.

The lad was halfway to the door when he turned, his face a mask of worry. "Well, maybe if I just came in there for a minute like," he said. "You promise not to try to escape?"

"With a man like you in here, why'd I want to escape?" Jessie said with a sly smile.

Then she watched as the boy retrieved the keys off the desk and started toward her. So focused was her concentration on the set of keys in the boy's hand that she didn't see Quimby enter the room.

"What you doing, boy!" Quimby roared from the door.

137

The lad whirled, panicked. "Nothing, nothing, I was just . . . ," he stuttered.

Quimby crossed the room in two steps and snatched the keys out of his hand. "Nothing, was it?" he shouted. "You weren't fixing to release her, were you?"

"No, no, nothing like that," the youth said, backing away. "She was just gonna, I mean, I was gonna . . ."

"You were gonna release my prisoner, isn't that what you mean?" Quimby shouted, then struck the lad on the side of the head with his fist.

The blow silenced the boy as he was about to say something else, and sent him to the floor.

"There wasn't no call for that," the sheriff said. "Leave him be!"

But Quimby ignored him, his black rage still directed at the lad. He kicked out and caught the boy in the gut with his booted toe. "Release my prisoner, will you?"

"Stop it!" Jessie shouted, but Quimby ignored her, kicking out savagely at the boy again, this time hitting him high in the chest and drawing a gasping scream from him.

The boy was crawling now, head down, wheezing, disoriented and heading for the door. Quimby kicked him again, knocking the breath from him and sending him rolling on his side.

"You quit on that now!" the sheriff said.

In answer, Quimby kicked the boy yet again, cracking his ribs. The lad was in bad shape now, a thin line of foaming blood forming at his lips.

From her cell, Jessie saw that Quimby's face had been transformed into a mask of eye-popping, beet-red hate. His hands curled like claws at his side as he advanced on the youth.

"Stop it, now!" the sheriff ordered.

138

And Quimby kicked the boy again, but with little effect. The youth just seemed to roll over, gasping in shallow, ragged breaths.

"Stop!" Jessie called, but Quimby ignored her; his rage was focused on the lad. She could see it in his face, that he intended to kick the boy to death.

Then the sheriff went for his gun. Quimby caught the flash of movement from the corner of his eye and drew first, bringing the sheriff up short. "Don't do it," he said, breathing hard, eyes still wild.

The boy crawled, moaning and wheezing, away to a corner, where he collapsed, cowering.

"You can't do this. I'm the law," the sheriff protested as he brought his hand reluctantly away from his holster.

The large man was calming down now, the possessed madness draining from his eyes. He seemed to forget all about the boy. "The law, you're not the law," he said, regaining his composure. "The law is the fella with the gun, and I ain't sorry to say that right now that ain't you."

The room stood still for a long time. Quimby's panicked eyes searched the place, as if for escape. When he looked over to the boy, he saw the same thing that they all did, that the lad might die. Finally, he addressed the sheriff, "Drop that gunbelt and move over here. I'm taking my prisoner out of here."

The lawman did as he was told. Quimby retrieved the gunbelt and motioned the sheriff over to the boy. "You pick him up, put him in that cell."

"There ain't no need for this, none at all," the sheriff said, his hands raised.

"I'll tell you what there's a need for and what there ain't no need for," came the answer.

Once again the sheriff did as he was told and dragged the lad over to the cell. Quimby threw the sheriff the keys, then searched the cabinet along the wall. He found what he was looking for in a lower drawer.

"Put him in the cell, then put these on her," he ordered, tossing over the heavy irons. "Bind her hands good. Take a turn round her waist with that chain. Be quick about it."

It was then that Quimby's two men appeared in the door, hung over from a night of drinking and whoring. They looked at their boss curiously, but did not comment.

"Bring those horses round," Quimby said. "And bring Dobbs's chestnut for the girl."

"I thought we were taking the stage," one of the men said timidly.

"Well, we ain't," Quimby said. "Now do it!"

The men vanished out the door.

When the sheriff had finished chaining Jessie, he stepped away to tend to the lad. "Damn, you busted his ribs in," he said. "He can't hardly breathe."

Quimby walked over to the cell. "He ain't gonna need to breathe if he's dead," he said. "Now sit!"

The lawman sat on the floor as Quimby tied him with a length of rope, then gagged him with a flour sack. When he was finished with the sheriff, he yanked Jessie forward by the cuffs.

Jessie resisted, pulling back, but Quimby brought the gun up under her chin. "I can shoot you so you'll live a day or two," he said. "Put you on a horse, it'll hurt so bad you'll beg me to kill you. That how you want to ride out?"

She had no doubt that he'd do it and didn't resist the next time he pulled at the chains. "You can't hope to get away with this," she said. "Don't you think they'll come after you?"

"Then you'll pardon me all to hell if I don't sit round and wait for them," Quimby answered, closing the cell door on the dying lad and the trussed-up sheriff and marching Jessie forward toward the street.

Outside it was morning. A few wagons rolled down the street, miners and ranchers in for supplies. Quimby's two men were waiting at the edge of the boards, looking anxious and worried.

Quimby got up on a horse, and one of the men came down and helped Jessie up. It wouldn't be an easy ride, not with her hands chained tight to her waist.

"Now, you listen to me," Quimby said, in a harsh whisper. "One word on the way out of town. One look in the wrong direction and you will regret it."

As they rode out down the main street, Jessie between the two men and Quimby alongside, Jessie noticed the blank, curious stares from those they passed. Several times she thought of crying out, but knowing that Quimby would keep his promise, she held her tongue.

She didn't know where they were heading, but suspected that it was to Ames and that he needed her alive. That alone would buy her some time.

On a hill overlooking town, Ki, Slyke, and Dorry watched as the four men rode the trail north.

"That's them, has to be," Dorry said.

Ki nodded in agreement.

"Ki, that's one helluva story you told me last night," Slyke said. "I just hope it's true."

"It is true," Ki said. "Remember, you told half of it."

"Stop arguing; let's go get that lady," Dorry said.

"No, we must stick to the plan," Ki said. "We must discover who is behind this, though I suspect it is Mr. Jonathan Ames."

"Besides, if we tried now, they'd more than probably kill her," Slyke said.

141

"They would," Ki said with confidence.

"And it wouldn't be the first time. Anyone who ever got in the way of Starbuck and Ames Mining seemed to die, suddenlike. I don't see a Starbuck being an exception," Slyke replied. "That Ames, he's a big enough man in this territory, but he ain't right. All this time I've been blaming Starbuck. Big outfit like that, I figured it was crooked."

"It was an investment for Miss Starbuck," Ki said. "Purchased through a Chicago agent."

"I wouldn't have figured it that way," Slyke mused. "But I'm sorry enough as it is, not believing her when she told me who she was. Just sorry as hell."

"It is of no consequence now," Ki said. "But we must follow the plan."

Then the three of them walked back to the horses. Dorry's had been shot properly the night before and replaced now with one of Slyke's team. They rode back to the main trail and followed it for two miles. Jessie's captors would be careful to watch for anyone following for the first few miles; then their caution would diminish with each passing mile. This was what Ki was counting on. What he was betting Jessie's life on. Very simply, if he were wrong, she would die.

They rode at a steady trot for two miles, until reaching the first divide in the road. Then they pointed the horses up the trail. Dorry went back down and cleared the tracks. She returned just in time, as Quimby and his men passed.

★

Chapter 17

"They'll hang you," Jessie said. "You and your men here."

Quimby looked over at her and smiled. "They got to catch us first," he said. "With what your friend Ames is paying for this job, and for what extra he's gonna pay, we can disappear. Utah, Oregon, hell, Mexico, even."

Jessie noticed that the men weren't smiling all that much. Perhaps they didn't share Quimby's faith in Ames's largess. "You can't hide there," she said. "They'll be after you. Pinkertons, federal marshals, Ki. You can't hide from them."

Quimby guffawed. "We ain't done nothing," he said. "Missy, you're dead as dirt. Old Ames buried you yesterday. Telegraphed all the papers. Big doings. We kill you now, right now, nobody'll ever know."

"You mind telling me what exactly is behind all of this?" she asked.

"Miss Starbuck, you are," Quimby said, putting on a bad Boston accent. "You exactly are behind it. And it would have gone fine, too, if you hadn't decided to stick your pretty nose into the business. You shoulda just stayed in Texas and counted the money that Ames

143

sent you. That's all you shoulda done. But that wasn't enough for you."

"Tell me, what was Ames getting out of all this?" Jessie asked. "Besides the Starbuck name?"

"Well, it was prettiest thing you ever saw . . . ," one of the men began, before Quimby silenced him with a glance.

"I think you better hear that directly," Quimby said. "It ain't that I don't know, it's just I know how much he would surely appreciate telling you himself. Ames, if there's one thing you can say about him, he likes to brag. That's his short-fall you might say. On the other hand, he never brags to people who might live more than three or four minutes. Now, that's a virtue I can appreciate in a man."

They stopped twice during the day to rest and water the horses. Quimby, it appeared, was not in any hurry to get where he was going. By late afternoon they had turned off the main road, onto an old mining trail. Jessie, who'd been working at a button of her blouse for the last two hours, dropped it as they made the turn.

Twenty-five yards up the steep slope, the main road vanished behind the trees.

"So, we're not going to Gold Hill?" Jessie asked, speaking louder than she had to.

"Hell no," one of the men answered. "That's about the last place we'd be taking you."

"Shut it," Quimby ordered. "And you, too, Miss Starbuck."

The trail continued upward, twisting along the side of the hill, the ground all but obscured by deadfall and weeds. It was dusk when they turned again, this time into the trees. Quimby paused, getting his bearings, then continued on. A few hundred yards up the rocky slope, they came to a narrow gulley carved deep by

144

spring rain. A horse couldn't turn sideways in it.

"This is it," Quimby said, walking his horse down a break in the gulley to its dry bed. When he reached bottom, he seemed to disappear beneath the rim.

The others followed, silently, their horses hesitant, then struggling for purchase on the rocky, root-tangled slope.

Ki, Slyke, and Dorry followed the tracks as best they could in the diminishing light. Ki estimated that Quimby didn't have more than a half mile lead on them. Yet just as the last light was fading from the sky, the tracks vanished completely.

Slyke stepped down off his horse and walked back a few yards. Carefully, he traced the line of fresh tracks to the left side of the road.

When he looked up questioningly, Ki came down off his horse. "They turned off," Slyke said, motioning with one finger as he rose up.

"What is up there?" Ki asked, then bent down to retrieve a tiny copper button. It could be no one else's but Jessie's. He recognized it from the shirt she had worn during the train robbery.

"Indian trails, mining roads," Slyke said, taking the button Ki offered and examining it. He, too, recognized it. "All crisscrossed to hell and back. Like a cobweb. It's what I was afraid they'd do, head up in there. Be like trying to find fly shit in a pile of pepper."

"We go," Ki said.

"At night? We won't see nothin'," Dorry put in, but spurred her horse forward anyway.

"If we're gonna do it, we might as well, 'stead of talking about it," Slyke said as he climbed back on his horse.

When the trail grew too narrow, Ki came down off his horse and walked before the group. By then it was full dark and impossible to go farther.

"We ain't doing no good stumbling around like this," Slyke said. "Best we can hope for is not to cripple a horse in the dark."

"I agree," Ki said. Looking down, he could barely see his feet under him, much less anything like tracks. "We camp here."

"There ain't nothing here," Dorry said. "No water, nothing."

"Here's as good as any place we're likely to find," Slyke said and got down off his horse. "Off the trail a bit."

They led the horses between the trees, where there was a bit of grass, and ground-staked them. They would worry about watering them properly tomorrow.

They had their bedrolls down when Dorry pulled out the fancy lamp. "Do not light it," Ki said. "We do not know how close they may be."

"They're probably over the hill and gone," Dorry answered, but did not light the lamp.

"Now, where the hell you going?" Slyke asked as Ki picked up his staff and began to walk off.

"To scout the area," he said.

"Why the hell not?" Slyke answered.

As Ki receded silently in the darkness, Dorry, lying on her side, turned to Slyke. "You know, friend," she said. "You just look real familiar to me."

"That a fact?" Slyke answered, without interest.

"That's what it is, all right," Dorry said, studying his dim features in the dark. "Where you from?"

"Me, I'm from around here," Slyke answered.

"Hell, nobody's from around here," she said with certainty. "You ever been up around Gold Hill?"

"One night is all," Slyke said.

"How 'bout Candalaria?" she asked.

"Nope."

"Aurora?"

"Never."

"Fernley?"

"No, ma'am."

"How 'bout Hazen, Thompson, Ludwig, Sodaville? Ever get down to Rhyolite?"

"Can't say that I have."

"You don't get around much, do you?"

Slyke rolled over, feigning sleepiness. "Maybe you get around too much."

"Now, that there, that's another fact," she said, relenting for the time being, but not giving up.

Ki walked silently into the trees, listening. At first he could hear only the vague whispering of Dorry and Slyke; then, a hundred yards or so to the north, he heard the sound of water. It was a timid splashing close by. He crept forward, careful of his steps, raising the staff up off the ground.

Then he saw him, a lone man, standing before a tree, in the process of relieving himself.

Ki came forward as the man turned, and before the man could take a step, he brought the staff up, holding it in the center of the broad back. The man froze.

"Do you know what this is?" Ki asked in a whisper.

When the man started to say something, Ki whispered, "Just nod."

The man nodded.

Stepping forward, Ki lifted the revolver from the man's holster and pulled the knife from his belt sheath. "Turn around, please," Ki said. "Quietly."

The man turned to see his own gun pointed at him. And worse, he saw he'd been fooled by a broom or hoe handle.

147

"Be so kind as to walk now," Ki said. "If you call out, I will shoot."

The man began walking, Ki moving him in the right direction by a touch now and again with the gun.

As they walked into the camp, Slyke sprang awake, eyes wide at the sight. Dorry, not quite yet asleep, rose also.

"What you find there, Ki?" Slyke asked.

"They are nearby," Ki said. "Very close."

"Could have let him tuck himself in before marching him round in the wilderness and all," Dorry said.

It was then that Ki realized that the man had been taken by surprise and had not had time to return his privates to his pants.

"I'm gonna put my hands down, just for a minute," the man said, lowering his hands.

"Pull yourself together there," Dorry said. "Ain't nobody here interested in what you're showing off."

"Yes, ma'am," the outlaw replied and buttoned his pants.

Slyke rose and approached the man. "Now that we got that little matter put away," he said. "Where they taking that Starbuck gal?"

"I tell you that, Quimby'll kill me," the man said.

"You don't tell us, I'm likely to kill you," Slyke answered.

The outlaw thought it over for a second, then reached his decision. All at once he began to scream. But the word, which Ki thought might have been "Quimby," came out like a gargled cry as Ki landed a striking blow with the *bo* across the outlaw's skull. The man fell to the ground, unconscious.

"You're just mighty handy with that stick, ain't you?" Slyke asked, amazed at the speed with which Ki had landed the blow.

148

"What're we gonna do with him?" Dorry asked, turning the outlaw's head sideways with the toe of her shoe.

"Tie 'im up," Slyke said. "We can ask him again when he wakes up."

★

Chapter 18

Something was wrong. Jessie could sense it. First, one of the men wandered off and didn't return; then Quimby and the remaining man conferred in hushed tones well away from her. The argument ended when the man raised his voice, but before he could say anything, Quimby knocked him down with a fist to the gut.

"Only reason I don't kill your miserable ass is I may need you later on," Quimby said.

"He's going to kill you anyway," Jessie said, speaking up. "Kill you or get you killed, either one."

"You shut your mouth," Quimby roared, pointing a finger at Jessie. "One more word from you, Miss Starbuck, you'll see just how mean life can get!"

Jessie closed her mouth, content that she had already planted a seed in the outlaw's head. She didn't know where the other one had gone to; it didn't make sense that he wouldn't take his horse or gear. But fear might have been guiding him. And fear, she knew, was a powerful force. Maybe even more powerful than greed or hate.

She slept fitfully, awakening often to test the

chains. Then, sometime before dawn, she awakened again. There was movement farther down the gully. Someone was climbing, scraping dirt from the side. Then she saw him, the remaining henchman, scrambling up the slope, his saddlebags draped over his shoulder, his gun out.

Quimby stirred, freezing the man in his tracks, then went back to snoring.

The man continued the climb up the steep slope, his hands grasping desperately for holds on the dried dirt and roots. When he was just about over, Quimby sprang to his feet. The man, half out of the gully, couldn't turn to shoot; rather he kept scrambling.

"You lily-hearted son of a bitch," Quimby snarled as he pulled the man back down into the trench.

The man fell hard, landing on his back as Quimby snatched the gun from his hand. "Oh, you bastard, you coward!" Quimby sputtered, completely consumed by rage.

For an instant, it looked as if Quimby would shoot the man with his own gun, then inexplicably, he tossed it away. "Shooting's too damn good for you, understand?"

The man rose to his feet slowly, hands out in front, in an attitude of total surrender. Quimby hit him, then snapped his head back and sent him sprawling against the wall.

"D. G., no, no," the man tried, pleading.

And Quimby hit him again, spreading his nose across his face.

Jessie came to her feet and charged. She'd be damned if she'd sit back and watch this animal beat a man to death. When she hit him, it was with a high kick that landed square in the big man's gut.

Quimby went down and Jessie moved in, but before she could kick again, he had his gun out. "You just step

152

back, back off, lady," he said, panting. "This is none of your concern. None at all."

The big man raised the gun, as if to shoot the other outlaw, but instead he struck it butt-first against the man's mouth, uprooting a half dozen teeth.

The man babbled, spit blood, and charged. Quimby struck him again with the revolver, across the top of the head, caving his skull in.

He lay motionless, facedown on the ground, for a long time, his breath gurgling blood in his throat. Then very slowly he got to his knees. Even in the darkness, Jessie could see the man's eyes riding high up in his head, showing plenty of white. By now he probably didn't even know what was happening or where he was.

Quimby waited until the man was almost to his feet, then struck him again. He fell over, with a timid grunt. "Can't even fight proper, you worthless sack of shit," Quimby hissed. "Get on your feet."

Amazingly, the man summoned the strength to rise. Perhaps, somewhere deep down, he thought that it might save his life. He was wrong. Before he reached his knees, Quimby kicked out, snapping the man's head sideways and breaking his neck. The man fell over dead in a heap.

Quimby wasn't even breathing hard. "Good help's hard to find, Miss Starbuck," he said, an evil grin spreading across his face. "They just die to easy. Look at a man wrong, he's just as likely to fall over dead."

"You're a damned butcher," she spit.

"Maybe, Miss Starbuck," he answered. "That may well be, but you're the one going to market."

"We know where they got her, let's just go get her out," Dorry said.

"We cannot," Ki answered softly.

"That Quimby'll kill her real quick," Slyke said. "Kill her to save his own hide."

They were gathered in a small circle, their prisoner tied tightly, off to one side.

Slyke rose, unholstering his gun, and walked over to the bound man. "I'm gonna ask you but once more," he said, kneeling down to pull off the gag. "Where they taking Miss Starbuck?"

For answer, the man spit in Slyke's face. "Go to hell," he said, a smirk spreading across his mouth.

Slyke lifted the gun slightly, placing it between the man's eyes, then wiped the spittle off his face with a sleeve. "You're a pretty tough hombre, ain't you?" he said. "Pretty tough."

"Not afraid of a bullet," came the answer.

"No, I don't s'pose you would be," Slyke said. "Probably had your share of women."

"That's truth," the man said with a smile.

"Liquor, too, I s'pose."

"I drank some," the man answered, still grinning.

"Probably raised all kinds of hell," Slyke said. "Feel you got your fair share all around."

"Kill me now, I wouldn't complain."

Slyke pulled the hammer back and cocked his head. "Wouldn't take much to save your miserable life," he said. "Just a word."

"You gonna kill me, kill me," came the answer.

Slyke eased his finger off the trigger and thumbed the hammer back into position. Then he got up and walked over to Ki and Dorry. "That one ain't gonna talk," he said. "Doesn't care whether he lives or dies."

"You know, I got myself an idea," Dorry said. "I think I can get him talking."

"How?" Ki asked in a whisper.

154

"Just you give me ten minutes with him," she said, then began digging in her bags. When she returned, she was holding her fancy lamp, a straight razor, a canteen, and a shaving mug.

"You are going to shave him?" Ki asked.

"My daddy was a barber," she said, then walked over to the man.

The outlaw stared in disbelief as she approached. "Now, what all are you about?" he asked.

"Figured as long as they were gonna kill you, you might as well go out clean-shaven."

"I don't want no shave," he said, watching as she lit the lamp.

"You ain't got no choice," she answered, kneeling down to mix a little water in the mug. Then she foamed up the shaving powder with two fingers.

"What you up to?" the man asked.

"Told you, just a shave," she said, straddling his legs.

"Don't want a shave," he said.

"No damn choice," she said, applying the lather to his week-old growth.

Ki and Slyke watched, stunned as she lathered him up good. Then with a flick of her wrist, she opened the razor. It shone brightly in the lamplight.

"See, my daddy was a barber," she said, running the razor over his neck. "Shaved him from the time I was a little girl."

When the razor had a full helping of suds on it, she wiped it smoothly across his bound arm.

The outlaw's eyes were wide, filled with disbelief and fear.

"Now, my daddy, he told me this, and I believe him," Dorry said, easing the razor again up the neck. "Told me that no matter how brave a man is, put him in a chair and a stranger with a razor over him, he's

155

gonna be afraid. Just a little. You afraid?"

"Not a you," came the timid reply.

The razor flew out toward his neck in a quick flash, and the gunman froze, his eyes shutting tight as Dorry neatly cut the rag from around his neck. "That's good then," she said, smiling. "Because a lot of men are scared. See this big old vein here, on the side a your neck. Cut that, you're a dead man. Bleed and spurt like a butchered hog. I seen it, plenty of times." To emphasize her point, she laid the razor right against the vein, tapping it lightly.

The outlaw's eyes widened.

Dorry began shaving his left cheek. The outlaw closed his eye. "My daddy, he was a good man. Liked to drink, though," she said. "And drinking and barbering, well, they don't mix. See, fella had his eye closed, just like you got. Keep it closed and I'll show you. Well, my daddy slipped, cut his lid open, neat as you please."

To illustrate, she placed the edge of the razor against his eyelid. "Pure miracle, he didn't blind the fella," she added. "But just a little twitch, man had half a lid left. Didn't last long. Heard his eye dried up like an old apple. I don't like to think about it."

Then, very slightly, she twitched. "Oops," she cried out in an oddly girlish voice as a thin line of blood formed on the lid. "Well, that ain't too bad. I seen worse."

The outlaw was frozen now, one bleeding eye closed, the other wide with panic.

"I'm not too heavy for you, am I?" she asked, wiggling a little as she worked the razor up his cheek.

He shook his head, just slightly.

"People, don't realize, barber sees his share of blood," she said, wiping off more suds. "Even good ones." Then she was working her way up around his ear. She was holding the ear out, just a little, when she said, "Oops," again. "Oh, now, look what I've done."

But the sharp jolt of pain that ran through the gunman had already told him. He didn't need to have her hold the tiny bit of flesh out for him to see. "Stop it," he said. "Please."

"Now, you wait, mister," she answered. "I'm gonna shave you good. Just let me use this here gag to stop the bleeding."

She continued shaving him for a long time without blood or incident. Finally, she said, "You know, what's interestin', what they do to unfaithful women down in Mexico. They cut them across the lip." She placed the razor gently across the outlaw's upper lip.

"Just cut down," she continued. "Right on through till it clicks on the teeth. Leaves a white little scar when it heals up. Funny thing to do, doncha think?"

"I seen that," the outlaw answered, his voice weakened.

"My daddy, though, he was mean sometimes when he was drinking," she said. "One time he was drinking and man came in, Mr. Simon. Funny sort of fella. Man never smiled. People said he performed unnatural acts with his chickens. Imagine that?"

The outlaw shook his head.

"Anyway, Mr. Simon, he owed my daddy money, not much, but enough so my daddy worried 'bout it," Dorry said. "Right off, Mr. Simon and Daddy went at it again, arguing over money. Know what my daddy did? Called Mr. Simon 'a grim-faced bastard' and cut right through his lip, side to side. Doctor tried sewing it up, but the lip just turned all purply puslike and kinda rotted off his face, right off the thread. Looked like cat whiskers. Anyway, he always smiled-like after that."

"Your daddy sounds like he had some different ideas," the outlaw said.

"Now, don't say nothing about my daddy. He taught me everything I know. How to shave, for one," Dorry warned. "Know what else? I heard 'bout a barber in the Indian territories, cut out a tumor."

The gunman didn't say anything; he was too concerned with the way she was waving the razor around in front of him.

"Know where that tumor was?" she asked. "Bet you can't guess."

He shook his head, very slightly.

"It was on this fella's eye," she answered, bringing the edge of the razor within a hair of his right eye. "Imagine that, cutting out a tumor with a razor?"

This time he didn't answer the question. The razor glinted in front of his opened eye.

"You don't have no tumors, do you?" she asked.

From deep in his throat he said, "No."

"I would purely like to try that," she said, moving the blade just a little closer. "What with you gonna die and all. Just sort of try to flick out that bad old tumor. Flick it on out!" She flicked the razor from eye to eye.

The gunman let out a whimpering cry as she opened a small nick, just below the eyebrow.

All told, it was just about the longest shave that Ki, or Slyke for that matter, had ever seen. Dorry just stayed perched on the outlaw's lap, talking and scraping at his face with a razor. Every once in a while, she'd slice off a small piece, just to make certain he was paying attention. At the end of an hour, he was ready to talk.

★

Chapter 19

They came up on the abandoned mine before noon.
What was left of the operation stood in a clearing
abutting a wall of rock. It was the sorriest mining
operation that Jessie had ever seen.

The sluice off to the side was long abandoned, its
sides rotted through, the small spring that fed it long
dried up or re-routed. The shaft, whose entrance was
not even half-completed, stood as a black shadow
in the rocky hillside, not even boarded up, its support beams lying in a heap just inside. But someone
had had high hopes for the mine at one time. Piles
of narrow-gauge rail and ties rested in the clearing,
and an overturned ore cart had capsized nearby. A
bunkhouse and five-stall stable stood on one side,
their roofs collapsed in on their walls, while a small
shack stood on the other side. The shack was the only
structure that looked the least bit kept up.

"Recognize it?" Quimby asked as they entered the
clearing.

Jessie looked around more closely. In all, the place
looked as if nobody had set foot in it since before the
Comstock strike. "Should I?" she answered.

"Maybe you should," Quimby said with a laugh. "It's the Starbuck and Ames operation. Pulling out a hundred thousand a year in gold and silver from that shaft."

Jessie was thinking about that when a figure appeared in the door of the shack. It was Ames. He was wearing a fancy jacket and derby. He was smiling broadly in welcome.

"My dear departed partner, how good of you to come," he said, stepping off the porch of the shack. "The ride was not too tiring, I hope."

Quimby climbed down and tied his and Jessie's horses to the ore cart, then grabbed Jessie roughly down from the saddle.

"Careful, careful," Ames cautioned as Quimby pulled Jessie down.

Once Jessie had her feet on the ground, she broke free of Quimby's grasp and marched up to Ames. "Maybe you'd care to tell me what you've been up to here?" she demanded.

"My dear, just step inside," Ames said, still jovial. "Step inside and I shall explain everything."

Quimby came up and pushed Jessie forward.

"Easy, my good man," Ames scolded. "We wouldn't want her to fall, now would we?"

The inside of the shack was not what Jessie had expected. Far from matching the run-down exterior, it was spotless. A velvet chaise stood in one corner, just in front of a large canopied bed. The kind of gentle drawing-room art that Jessie detested hung on the walls, and a large carpet, thick as ungrazed grass, was spread out across the tightly calked floor. Someone had gone to a lot of trouble to haul all this up into the hills.

"Wine, my dear?" Ames asked, cordially. "I regret that I cannot offer you champagne. Though I do have an excellent sherry. And some very nice port."

Jessie lifted her manacled hands in answer.

"Pity, but I see you're restrained," Ames said, and poured himself a glass of tawny port from a crystal decanter.

"Just tell me the meaning of all this," Jessie said.

"The meaning, my dear, is money," Ames answered politely, then took a sip of the liquor. "But isn't that always the meaning?"

"For people like you maybe," Jessie shot back.

"Regardless," Ames said, dismissing the comment with an upraised palm. "This is the meaning. Having no real interest in the brutish work of mining, I devised what I like to think of as a rather brilliant business enterprise. You see, we let others actually extract the ore and nuggets from the dirt, then relieve them of it, just prior to sale. Having no real objection to commerce, we then sell it ourselves."

"Then why did you need me?" Jessie asked.

"We needed someone with an impeccable reputation. Who would have dreamed you'd actually venture to this remote outpost to inspect your investment?" Ames said. "The Starbuck name, however, carried with it the weight of respectability. This was particularly useful when we began to branch out, as it were. With the supply of precious metals diminishing, we began to, shall I say, acquire them in their refined state. Then very carefully return them to their crude beginnings for sale."

"The train robbery, for instance?" Jessie said.

"Perfect example." Ames beamed. "In addition to bringing you to us, it supplied several thousand in coins, watches, and the like for our enterprise. I might also add that I paid out a ransom of some five thousand dollars for your safe return. Alas, your body was found burned beyond recognition just outside Gold Hill. I

161

identified the personal effects myself."

"You killed some poor girl, just to fake my death?"

"It was a necessity," Ames said. "Naturally, you would have come here on your own volition and no doubt discovered our small deception. But the robbery was also an excellent opportunity to stage your death."

"Then why am I still alive?" Jessie said. "Why even bother bringing me here?"

"For these," Ames said and retrieved a fat stack of papers from a gold-trimmed desk. "If you'd be so kind as to step this way."

Jessie stepped away from Quimby, who stood near the door, and went over to the desk. Ames turned the pages of the documents as she read. The documents were letters, contracts, bills of sale. In total, the papers signed over all ownership of the mine to Ames for a supposed sum of just under two hundred thousand dollars. They had all been witnessed by a judge in Gold Hill. More remarkably, there was an application to file for a listing on the San Francisco Stock Exchange. That alone would bring in more money than any gold strike.

"I'd rather you just killed me now," Jessie said.

Ames set his drink down carefully and stepped back. Jessie noticed that his features had changed markedly. They had hardened with a grim determination. "I'm sure you would," he said. "A woman of your high principles. And you will die here. I'll not deceive you regarding that. The only question remaining is how you will die. Quickly, with a bullet in the head, or left to Mr. Quimby's expert imagination. Either way, you will sign those papers."

"Go to hell, Ames," Jessie said.

"Pity you should take that attitude," Ames answered easily. "Perhaps a night in the mine would help. Tomorrow, if your attitude hasn't improved, then I'll turn you over to Quimby here."

Quimby yanked her back by the chain around her waist, pulling her toward the door. As she was pulled out, she watched as Ames took another small sip of his port.

They were just outside the door when Jessie saw her chance. Pretending to stumble on the narrow porch, she fell facedown in the dirt. Quimby cursed as the chain slipped from his grasp, then bent toward her.

But Jessie was already rolling over, and as Quimby bent down, she kicked out, catching him with the heel of her boot at the point of his jaw. His head was jerked back, and she kicked again, this time landing a blow on his knee.

The fat man collapsed off the porch as Jessie leapt to her feet. Quimby went for his gun then, but Jessie was quicker, landing a solid blow between his legs, then kicking the gun from his grasp.

As Jessie jumped toward the firearm, Quimby yelled and reached for his boot. But Jessie was on the gun before he could get to the small hideout. Holding the big revolver in her chained hands, she sat upright and fired between her knees.

Quimby's hand exploded in a thick spray of blood and shattered bone. What was left, hanging on the end of a bloody stump, looked like scraps from a slaughterhouse floor.

The door of the shack flew open, and Ames, holding an English double-barreled 12-gauge, appeared. Jessie fired again, just over Quimby's head, and splintered the door frame near Ames, who vanished back inside.

In the time it had taken to fire at Ames, Quimby regained his feet. He took one step toward her, and Jessie shot again, hitting him in the gut. The shot halted the fat man, but just for a moment. He kept coming, his face twisted into a mask of animal hate.

Scrambling back, crablike, Jessie fired again. The shot hit the fat man on the belt, doubling him over. Jessie fired twice more, each time hitting the big man, but he kept coming, his chest a mass of blood and shredded flesh beneath his bullet-riddled clothes. Then the gun clicked on empty. Quimby fell, hands out. He came down across Jessie, pinning her to the ground as his cold hands sought her throat.

As she struggled under the considerable weight of the dying Quimby, she looked up to see Ames, standing over her, shotgun poised at her head. "You persisted until the last," he said.

Jessie could not answer Ames. Then suddenly she felt Quimby go still. He was dead.

"It seems you've eliminated one of my problems in any event," Ames said, and pulled the hammer of the shotgun back.

He was about to fire when another shot suddenly rang out. Ames stood there for a second, a gaping bullet hole in his neck, then dropped the shotgun. A moment later he followed it to the ground.

Lifting one knee, Jessie managed to roll the dead Quimby off her, just in time to see Ki, Slyke, and a woman emerge from the trees.

"You know something, Miss Starbuck," Slyke said, holstering his fancy Colt. "For such a pretty woman, you get yourself mixed up with the ugliest messes."

"Never mind that," Jessie said. "Just get these damn chains off me."

★
Chapter 20

They set out at dawn the next day and reached the main road in time to meet up with the sheriff and the four-man posse. They were heading back to town after a day and a night of fruitless searching.

"Miss Starbuck," the sheriff said, nudging his horse up alongside Jessie's and removing his hat. "Would appear I owe you an apology."

Jessie nodded back. It was too little and more than a little late. But she knew that it was the best the lawman could do.

"Fella in San Franciso sent up a picture of you," the sheriff said. "If it would have come a day sooner, maybe some of all this wouldn't have had to happen."

Then the lawman eyed the two dead men, Ames and Quimby, who were tied over horses held by Slyke. He nodded with a grim satisfaction. Then he cast a questioning look over to the live prisoner. "Boy, I don't know who tends to your barbering, but you would do a whole lot better to find someone else," the sheriff said, noticing the two dozen small scabbed-over wounds that covered his face.

"Crazy damned whore done it," the outlaw said without emotion. "Crazy damned whore."

Dorry smiled with something like satisfaction. She was wearing her purple dress with the small hat. And the sheriff nodded to her with a kind of awed and fearful respect.

"Well, I s'pose you folks got a story to tell," the sheriff said.

"It can wait, Sheriff. It can wait till we get back to town," Slyke put in.

"Just what I was gonna suggest," the lawman replied easily. "The very thing. I s'pose it can wait till tomorrow, when you folks are cleaned up and fed."

They were not halfway back to the small town when Slyke let his horse drift back to where Dorry was riding. He looked over at her with a small, satisfied smile. "How you holding up there?" he asked.

"Better than fair," she said. "Just better than fair."

Jessie pulled up lightly on the reins and joined them. "I'm heading back to Texas," she said. Then added, "Me and Ki."

"I figured you would," Slyke said, a small note of disappointment in his face.

"We'll need someone to look after the mine, clean up the mess," she said. "You can have the job, if you want it."

"What about me?" Dorry asked. "Me and Ki?"

"It's a two-person job," Jessie answered. "Mr. Slyke here is going to need some help."

Dorry arched an eyebrow. "What's it pay?"

"Now, that's between you and Mr. Slyke here," Jessie said. "You two work out the details between yourselves."

Slyke smiled broadly. "I think we can manage that."

Jessie spurred her horse forward to join Ki and the sheriff at the front of the line. As she moved by the

166

posse, she heard Dorry say, "I know you from some-wheres. Just can't put my finger on it. You know, maybe without that beard . . ."

"Kinda fond of this beard," Slyke answered a little defensively. "But you'll have some time to figure it out."

When Jessie was alongside Ki, she turned and asked, "You'll miss her, won't you?"

"Yes," he said. "She is a good woman."

They rode in silence for a long time, their horses easily negotiating the slight downward grade toward town and stepping easily between the deep ruts left by coaches and Washoe wagons. From off the distant desert a warm breeze was blowing, coming up scented through the big pines and carrying with it the hint of sage.

Jessie closed her eyes and thought of Texas.

Watch for

LONE STAR AND THE SAN DIEGO BONANZA

129th novel in the exciting LONE STAR series
from Jove

Coming in May!

SPECIAL PREVIEW

If you like Westerns, here's a special look at
an exciting new series.

On the razor's edge of the law,
one man walks alone . . .

DESPERADO

The making of an outlaw—the legend begins!

The following is an excerpt from this new
action-packed Western,
available now from Jove Books . . .

The wolf loped through the brush, moving soundlessly over the sandy soil. From time to time it stopped, testing the air, scanning its surroundings, listening. It was an old wolf, had grown old because of its caution, because of listening, watching, never showing itself. There once had been many wolves in the area, but most were gone now, most dead, killed by men with rifles, and traps, and poison. This particular wolf had long ago learned to avoid man, or anything that smelled of man. And it had survived.

It was late spring; the sagebrush still showed some green. The wolf had been eating well lately; many animals browsed on that green, and the wolf browsed on the animals, the smaller ones, the ones he could catch by himself. There were no longer any wolf packs to pull down bigger game: deer, antelope. Life was now a succession of small meals, barely mouthfuls.

The wolf was thirsty. A quarter of a mile ahead a patch of thicker green showed. A water hole. The wolf could smell the water. It increased its pace, loping along, bouncing on still-springy legs, tongue lolling from its mouth, yellow eyes alert.

173

A thicket of willows some fifteen feet high grew up on the far side of the water hole. The wolf gave them a cursory scan. It raised its nose, its main warning system, and could smell only water, willows, and mud.

It was late enough in the season for the water hole to have shrunk to a scummy puddle, no more than a foot deep and twenty feet across. In winter, when the rains came, the water formed a small lake. One more look around, then the wolf dropped its muzzle, pushed scum aside, and lapped slowly at the water. After half a minute the wolf raised its head again, turning it from side to side, nervous. The water had claimed its attention for a dangerously long time.

Suddenly, the wolf froze. Perhaps the horse had made a small movement. Horses do not like the company of wolves, yet this one had stood motionless while the wolf approached, held so by the man on its back. The wolf saw him then, the man, blending into the willow thicket, mounted, sitting perfectly motionless.

A moment's stab of fear, the wolf's muscles bunching, ready to propel him away. But the wolf did not run. Ears pricked high, it stood still, looking straight at the man, sensing that he meant it no harm. Sensing, in its wolf's brain, an affinity with this particular man.

Wolf and man continued to look at one another for perhaps a half a minute. Then the wolf, with great dignity, turned, and loped away. Within seconds it had vanished into the brush.

The man did not move until he could no longer see the wolf. Then, with gentle pressure from his knees, he urged the horse out of the willows, down toward the water hole, let it drink again. The horse had been drinking earlier, head down, legs splayed out, when the man had first seen the wolf, or rather, seen

174

movement, about a quarter of a mile away, a flicker of grey gliding through the chaparral. He was not quite sure why he'd backed his horse into the willows, why he'd quieted the animal down as the wolf approached. Perhaps he wanted to see if it could be done, if he could become invisible to the wolf. Because if he could do that, he should be able to become invisible to anything.

The wind had been from the wolf's direction. The horse's hoofs had crushed some water plants at the edge of the pool; they gave off a strong odor, masking the man's scent, masking the horse's. A trick old Jedadiah had shown him, all those years ago . . . let nature herself conceal you.

He'd watched as the wolf approached the water hole, made one last cursory check of its surroundings, then began to drink. A big, gaunt old fellow. The man wondered how the hell it had survived. Damned stockmen had done their best to exterminate every wolf within five hundred miles. Exterminate everything except their cows.

He was aware of the moment the wolf sensed his presence, knew it would happen an instant before it actually did. He watched the wolf's head rise, its body tense. But he knew that it would not run. Or rather, sensed it. No, more than that . . . it was as if he and the wolf shared a single mind, were the same species. Brothers. The man smiled. Why not? Both he and the wolf shared a way of life . . . they were both the hunter and the hunted.

The wolf was gone now, the moment over, and the man, pulling his horse's head up from the water before it drank too much, left the pool and rode out into the brush. And as he rode, anyone able to watch from some celestial vantage point would have noticed that he travelled pretty much as the wolf had travelled,

175

almost invisible in the brush, just flickers of movement as he guided his horse over a route that would expose him least, avoiding high ground, never riding close to clumps of brush that were too thick to see into, places that might conceal other men.

He rode until about an hour before dark, then he began to look for a place to make camp for the night. He found it a quarter of an hour later, a small depression surrounded by fairly thick chaparral, but not so thick that he could not see out through it.

Dismounting, he quickly stripped the gear from his horse, the bedroll and saddlebags coming off first, laid neatly together near the place where he knew he would build a small fire. He drew his two rifles, the big Sharps and the lighter Winchester, from their saddle scabbards, and propped them against a bush, within easy reach. The saddle came off next; he heard his horse sigh with relief when he loosened the girth.

Reaching into his saddlebags, the man pulled out a hackamore made of soft, braided leather. Working with the ease that comes from doing the same thing dozens of times, he slipped the bit and bridle off his horse, and replaced it with the hackamore. Now, the horse would be able to graze as it wished, without a mouthful of iron bit in the way. More importantly, if there was danger, if the man had to leave immediately, he would have some kind of head stall already on his horse. When trouble came, speed was essential, thus the hackamore, and the style of his saddle, a center-fire rig, less stable than a double rig, but easy to throw on a horse when you were in a hurry.

The man fastened a long lead rope to the hackamore, tied the free end to a stout bush, then left his horse free to move where it wanted. He allowed himself a minute to sink down onto the sandy ground, studying the area around him, alert, but also aware of the peacefulness of the place. There was no sound at all except the soft movement of the warm breeze through the bushes, and, a hundred yards away, a single bird, singing its heart out.

In the midst of this quiet the man was aware of the workings of his mind. He was comfortable with his mind, liked to let it roam free, liked to watch the way it worked. He had learned over the years that most other men were uneasy with their minds, tried to blot them out with liquor or religion.

His gaze wandered over to his horse. To the hackamore. He remembered the original Spanish word for halter . . . *Jaquima*, altered now by the Anglo cowboy. Through his reading, and he read a great deal, the man had discovered that many of the words the Western horseman used were of Spanish origin, usually changed almost beyond recognition. When the first American cowboys came out West, they learned their trade from the original Western settlers, the Spanish *vaqueros*. Matchless horsemen, those Spaniards, especially out in California. God they could ride!

When the Anglos moved into Texas, it was the local Mexicans who'd taught them how to handle cattle in those wide open spaces. Yet, he knew that most cowboys were totally unaware of the roots of the words they used every day. Not this man. He liked to think about words, about meanings, mysteries. He had an unquenchable hunger to learn.

And at the moment, a more basic hunger. There was movement off to his left; a jackrabbit, one of God's stupider creatures, was hopping toward him. The rabbit stopped about ten yards away, then stood up on its hind legs so that it could more easily study this strange-smelling object. Rabbit and man were both immobile for several seconds, watching one another, then the man moved, one smooth motion, the pistol on his hip now in his hand, the hammer snicking back, the roar of a shot racketing around the little depression.

Peering through a big cloud of white gunsmoke, the man thought at first he had missed; he could not see the rabbit. But then he did see it, or what was left of it, lying next to a bush a yard from where it had been sitting when he'd fired. He got up, went over to the dead rabbit. The big .45 caliber bullet had not left much of the head or front quarters, but that didn't matter. The hind quarters were where the meat was.

It took him less than five minutes to skin and gut the rabbit. He methodically picked out the big parasitic worms that lived beneath the rabbit's scruffy hide, careful not to smash them, and ruin the meat. Ugly things. It took another fifteen minutes to get a fire going, and while the fire burned down to hot coals, the man whittled a spit out of a springy manzanita branch, and ran it through the rabbit.

It was dark before the rabbit was cooked. After seeing those worms, the man wanted to make sure the meat was done all the way through. He ate slowly, trying not to burn his fingers. For dessert he fished a small can of peaches out of his saddlebags. His only drink was warm, brackish water from his canteen. But he considered the meal a success, not so much because of the bill of fare, but because of the elegance of his surroundings: the pristine cleanness of the sandy ground on which he sat, the perfume of the chaparral, the broad band of the Milky Way arching overhead, undimmed.

Yeah, he thought, pretty damned beautiful. He scratched his chin through a week's unshaven bristle. And reflected that his life was damned lonely sometimes. Well, that was a choice he'd made, way back, and he was a man who stuck with his decisions.

Still, it could get damned lonely.

A special offer for people who enjoy reading the best Westerns published today.

WESTERNS!

NO OBLIGATION

Mail the coupon below

To start your subscription and receive 2 FREE WESTERNS, fill out the coupon below and mail it today. We'll send your first shipment which includes 2 FREE BOOKS as soon as we receive it.

Mail To: **True Value Home Subscription Services, Inc. P.O. Box 5235 120 Brighton Road, Clifton, New Jersey 07015-5235**

YES! I want to start reviewing the very best Westerns being published today. Send me my first shipment of 6 Westerns for me to preview FREE for 10 days. If I decide to keep them, I'll pay for just 4 of the books at the low subscriber price of $2.75 each; a total $11.00 (a $21.00 value). Then each month I'll receive the 6 newest and best Westerns to preview Free for 10 days. If I'm not satisfied I may return them within 10 days and owe nothing. Otherwise I'll be billed at the special low subscriber rate of $2.75 each; a total of $16.50 (at least a $21.00 value) and save $4.50 off the publishers price. There are never any shipping, handling or other hidden charges. I understand I am under no obligation to purchase any number of books and I can cancel my subscription at any time, no questions asked. In any case the 2 FREE books are mine to keep.

Name _____

Street Address _____ Apt. No. _____

City _____ State _____ Zip Code _____

Telephone _____

Signature _____
(if under 18 parent or guardian must sign)

Terms and prices subject to change. Orders subject
to acceptance by True Value Home Subscription
Services. Inc.

11083